The Holy Grail Code

Ehud Peled

Producer International Distributor
eBookPro Publishing
www.ebook-pro.com

The Holy Grail Code
Ehud Peled

Translation: Sharon Singer
Contact: peledu46@gmail.com

ISBN 9798373918114

The Holy Grail Code

Ehud Peled

Preface

Was the Holy Grail in fact flown to the Vatican packed in a brown briefcase? Where is it hidden today? And will it ever be revealed to the public eye?

The diligent investigative reporter Ilana Peres and the senior Police officer Victor Elbar kept their promise to one another and met over a cup of coffee. Though pleasant and relaxed, the conversation offered no help in solving the mystery.

Ilana eventually realized that the secret of the Grail is not the main mystery in this strange affair. She tried once again to find Dina, the technician from the genetics lab at the Technion, but she had disappeared without a trace.

Ilana thought to herself that if it was indeed the Son of God who drank from the goblet at "the last supper," then it would be a thousand times better for the secret to remain buried forever. Juicy myths are much more powerful and long-lasting than simple dry facts.

So, where and who keeps the data and strange symbols that dotted the sheets of paper coughed out by the genetic laboratory's computer and that rose to the sky in smoke and flames?

Perhaps it is buried in the most secret and secured vault in the State of Israel, next to the secret code that would be used to activate the nuclear device (possessed, according to foreign sources, by Israel), and one cannot possibly imagine which of these codes, in universal historical terms, has the greater potential for causing damage: the physical-chemical – or the biological-divine.

A Fighter Jet Falls from the Sky

On Sunday, August 21ˢᵗ, 2022, around noon, two fighter jets took off from Ramat David Airforce Base. The two planes circled at a high altitude over the Western Galilee as they practiced navigation and target detection.

It was one of the hottest days of the year and the two planes, chasing each other's tails, looked like small black dots in the sky.

Suddenly the muffled sound of an explosion rolled from the sky while a small flame burst from the tail of one of the jets. Due to what would later be determined as a "technical fault combined with human error," one of the planes went into a tailspin and crashed on a desolate hill east of Highway 70, near the town of Shfaram, drilling a large crater as it hit the solid ground.

2

Five Graves

For over a decade now, Ilana Peres has been presenting her TV program: "As a Matter of Fact." Based on extensive research, Ilana's programs deal with unusual facts and strange incidents. That evening, Ilana, well-groomed and eloquent as always, begins her show with a somewhat dramatic tone:

Ilana: "Good evening. For over ten years now, I have been presenting this program. Though our programs usually bring you strange and unusual events, tonight's story is unlike anything we have ever done before. The story we will be bringing to you tonight is indeed strange, incredible, and borderline fanciful.

"It all started a few weeks ago. Our team of investigators received scraps of rumors about five mysterious funerals, held in a Kibbutz cemetery in the Western Galilee."

Kibbutz Ramat Hatzafon Cemetery

A deadly silence engrosses the small and well-kept cemetery of Kibbutz Ramat Hatzafon. The only sound heard is a slight whisper of the wind blowing in the tops of the pine and cypress trees. Ilana strolls down the gravel path, examining the headstones. She reaches five fresh graves grouped together on the outskirts of the grove. There are black, yet to be engraved plaques placed atop four of the graves, with lettering appearing in white chalk: "John Doe 23 August 2022." The fifth plaque reads "Jane Doe 23 August 2022."

Ilana brushes away a light strand of hair from her forehead, and turns to the camera:

"We are now in the cemetery of Kibbutz Ramat Hatzafon. As you can see, we have found five fresh graves. Four men and one woman. They were all buried on the same day, August 23, 2022. Are they victims of an unfortunate series of road accidents? Initially, that is what we thought. However, a brief investigation we conducted discovered that on Tuesday, August 23, 2022, the date inscribed on the burial signs, as well as the entire week preceding it, there were no car or work accidents involving five fatalities. The fact that the graves do not bear any names also speaks volumes. We met with Mr. Isaiah Shohat, the manager of this Kibbutz cemetery.

With tombstones standing in the background, Isaiah seems a bit mortified during the impromptu interview.

Ilana: "Are you the person in charge of the Kibbutz cemetery?"

Isaiah: "Indeed."

Ilana: "Why are these five graves on the outskirts of the grove?"

Isaiah: "This plot is intended for the burial of non-Jews."

Ilana: "Who are the five deceased buried here?"

Isaiah: "I don't know."

Ilana: "Are there other unnamed gravestones in this cemetery?"

Isaiah: "There is one grave of an unknown person who was killed in 1948 during the War of Independence."

Ilana: "Do you know the circumstances of these people's deaths?"

Isaiah: "No."

Ilana: "And it doesn't seem a bit strange to you to bury five people in your cemetery without knowing who they were?"

Isaiah: "I just work here. You can ask Eldad – the kibbutz manager."

4

In Eldad's Office

Early noon. The green patches and well-kept gardens of the Kibbutz seem deserted while all of its members are seated under their air conditioners, escaping the heat. On one of the pathways, Ilana approaches Henya, a short, tanned, slow-walking old Kibbutz member, carrying a five-tier tiffin lunch box.

Ilana: "Good afternoon. Could you please point me to the Kibbutz Manager's office?"

Henya: "If he's already left for lunch, he would be in the dining hall now, and if he hasn't left for lunch yet, you would probably find him in his office on the first floor of the two-story building."

Since all the houses in the Kibbutz were red-tiled bungalows, the two-story rectangular building with a flat roof stood out like a sore thumb. On the door of one of the rooms downstairs is fixed a small wooden sign reading: "Community Manager." Ilana knocks lightly on the half-open door and enters.

Ilana: "Good afternoon."

The manager looks up from a pile of papers. He immediately recognizes the person standing in front of him.

Eldad: "Ilana Peres!? What a surprise! Such an honor! What are you doing here? I am an avid fan of all your shows. The inquiry into the poor health of the wild animals pushed away from their natural habitat by urban renewal construction projects was a true masterpiece."

Ilana: "Thank you. I just came from your cemetery. I was there with Isaiah."

Eldad: "Yes, Isaiah... an excellent guy, but you know... a little...," the community manager moves his finger near his head in the familiar circular motion.

Ilana: "I understand. I wanted to talk to you about those five fresh graves."

Eldad: "Yes..." His kind tone is now spiced with notes of tension.

Ilana: "Do you know who is buried there?"

Eldad: "No. We bury 'outsiders' in our cemetery sometimes – that is, people who are not residents of the kibbutz. We own a license for that, of course. I mean, it's not a business, there are many expenses. We receive a one-time payment, and then we take care of gardening and maintenance for life, or rather death... you know what I mean."

Ilana: "And don't you feel strange burying five nameless people, without knowing a single thing about them?"

Eldad: "And if they were called Jacob or Zelig – would that mean I know anything about them? As soon as a client, if you can call it that, presents us with a death certificate and an official burial permit, we provide the service. We are an established cemetery, and everything is done by the book."

Ilana: "And who was the 'client', as you noted, in this case?"

Eldad clears his throat: "Under any circumstances, I am not supposed to disclose that information. It is a question of the deceased right to privacy. I'm sure you would understand. I can only tell you, in general, that the person who handled this matter was a Prime Minister's Office official."

Ilana: "Can you elaborate?"

Eldad: " Sorry. As far as I'm concerned, in order to have a burial, four conditions are required: First – a corpse. Second – a death certificate. Third – a burial license and approval, and fourth – payment. Beyond that, it's not my business to investigate who the deceased were and under what circumstances they died."

Ilana: "May I ask, just out of curiosity, how much you charge?"

Eldad: "Fifteen thousand Shekels plus VAT, including burial fees from the National Insurance. It covers the plot, digging, burial, a tombstone and ongoing maintenance. It's really not a business. We only do this in special cases. Mainly when it comes to burying people who weren't Jewish, or whose religion is unknown. As you probably know, cases like that can be problematic sometimes."

Ilana: "Yes. Thank you for your time."

Ilana gets up from her chair and extends her arm to shake Eldad's hand. The community manager picks up a business card from a small mesh basket on his desk and hands it to Ilana.

Eldad: "If it's really that important to you, this guy might be able to help you."

Ilana: "Who is he?"

Eldad: "A lawyer. He showed up here after the funeral. He too was asking for information. I didn't share with him anything that I didn't share with you. Perhaps he found out more details since then."

Ilana: "Thank you."

The two shake hands and say their goodbyes.

5
In the TV Studio

In the studio, Ilana continues to outline the story.

Ilana: "The first mystery that we addressed was the accident. An accident in which five people died can't be overlooked. To our surprise, we did not find any reports. Not in the press, not on television, and not even the police... The mystery was solved by chance. Our investigator Yigal Eshet will share with us his amazing findings right after these messages."

After a brief and not so creative series of commercials, Ilana returns to the screen.

Ilana: "We're back. At this point, we have more open questions than answers. Nevertheless, we decided to move ahead and run with this broadcast, in the hope that one of you, the viewers at home, will be able to help us shed some light on the obscurities we will be discussing tonight. In the meantime," Ilana gestures with her palm to a handsome, dark-haired man sitting next to her, "We sent Yigal, our investigator, to trace the mysterious accident in which four men and one woman were killed. Tell us, Yigal, what you found."

Yigal: "Actually, it turns out that in addition to the five dead, apparently there was also one injured person in the accident. A few days ago, I joined an interesting trip in the company of a young lawyer named Zeev Shuali."

6

Yigal and Shuali Taking a Ride

On one of the main streets of the Carmel neighborhood in Haifa, the young ambitious tort lawyer Zeev Shuali makes his way in a black lifted Jeep. He feeds off of the "eternal hunting grounds" aka, the Israeli roads system which is known to provide much sustenance to the legal system in general, and to lawyers specializing in property and bodily injury claims as a result of road accidents, in particular.

Atty. Shuali is what people would call a "lone wolf." However, on that day, Yigal an investigator for the TV program "As a Matter of Fact" is sitting by his side. Yigal had reached Shuali the day before when he dialed the number given to Ilana by the Community Manager of Kibbutz Ramat Hatzafon, and after explaining the nature of his inquiry... he asked to join him as part of an item to be aired, regarding "the plague of traffic accidents."

Atty. Shuali naturally relished the opportunity to gain such wide exposure with little investment on his part and invited Yigal to join him on a "routine drive."

His 4x4 280 horsepower jeep is equipped with several antennas as high as a Division Commander's vehicle, topped with a sophisticated radio, Atty. Shuali uses to tune in on all traffic police frequencies.

At that moment, Shuali picks up a message from the Zvulun police dispatcher.

Dispatcher: "Unit Five, what is your location? Over."

Patrol officer: "Dispatch, this is Five. By the Tel-Hanan ice cream shop."

Dispatcher: "Five, throw away your ice cream and go immediately to Yagur junction. There's been a bad accident."

Shuali does not need to wait for more reports. Being the experienced hound he is, all of his senses are heightened instantly. He makes an illegal U-turn in the middle of the street, turns up the volume on the receiver, and rushes toward the scene of the accident.

Another report comes in within minutes:

Patrol officer: "This is Five at the scene of an accident at Yagur junction. There are casualties. Call an ambulance."

Dispatcher: "Five, this is dispatcher. How many vehicles involved? How many casualties? How bad are they? Did you stop traffic?"

Patrol officer: "This is Five here. Two vehicles. One private car, one truck. Looks like there are three people wounded, one badly injured. Send an ambulance immediately and backup to help stop traffic."

Dispatcher: "The ambulance is on its way. Patrol units two and six are also on their way to you."

Within ten minutes, Shuali and Yigal arrive at the scene. Three police cars and an ambulance are already on site, flickering yellow, red, and blue lights. Officers and paramedics are busy tending to the injured and preparing for transferring them to a hospital. Shuali rolls the window down and quickly records the scene. He pulls out a camera with a telescopic lens followed by a video camera and takes pictures.

He grabs a notepad from behind the front visor and jots down details of the location of the collision and the license plate numbers of the cars involved while he turns on the tape recorder by his steering wheel: "August twenty twenty-two; Yagur Junction; Toyota Corolla number... Volvo truck..."

Another ambulance arrives howling and flashing. The paramedics load the casualties onto the two ambulances and take off. Shuali races behind them.

In the Jeep, Yigal turns to Shuali:

Yigal: "So, you are what they call an 'ambulance chaser?'"

Shuali: "I don't really like that term, but in principle, yes. I make a living representing victims of car accidents, or in the case of death, representing family members. I don't get my entire clientele like this, but it is definitely effective."

Yigal: "How many years have you been in this field?"

Shuali: "About five. Since I got my license to practice law."

Yigal: "And doesn't it get boring? after all, it's more of the same – an accident is an accident is an accident..."

Shuali: "As far as I'm concerned, an accident is not the end but rather the beginning of the story. It's a good way to make a living and sometimes also very interesting and challenging. You do get the occasional odd cases. Like last week I came across a police unit reporting that a plane had crashed north of Route 70, near the Shfaram intersection."

Yigal: "A plane?! And you went to the crash site?"

Shuali: "Of course."

Yigal's ears perk up: "And what did you see?"

Shuali: "When I arrived, a police patrol car was already blocking access to the scene. I drove the jeep off-road, to an observation point on a nearby hill. I could see a patch of black thorns, the result of the fire that had broken out, caused by the collision. I stood there and looked at the wreckage and all the mess. As you can see, I also have a video camera in my car with which I shoot the accidents I encounter. Here, this is the camera," Shuali points at the camera bag now lying on the back seat, "You can check it out yourself."

Yigal picks up the bag and pulls out the camera. After fidgeting with the buttons under Shuali's direction, images begin to flash on the screen before his eyes.

The screen shows the nose of a plane stuck in the ground. A broken wing lying at the side, debris scattered everywhere; flames being extinguished as firefighters spray jets of water at them. A command car arrives, and soldiers jump out to encircle the plane wreckage. A police car struggles up the hill. Bedouin boys and a girl with a herd of goats watch from a "safe distance." A vehicle with multiple antennas arrives at the scene from which senior Air Force officers step out.

Much commotion boils all around the aircraft. A helicopter lands nearby and a fully equipped commando squad jumps out from its door.

Shuali, with one eye on the road and one eye on the camera screen, explains: "Ok, what we have here now is the deployment of military forces as well as the firefighters working on extinguishing the flames. Here now, that's a helicopter landing. I believe this is "Search and Rescue Unit – 669," they specialize in rescuing pilots."

Yigal, running through the scenes: "and what's happening now?"

Shuali: "Well, as you can see, it's already after sundown at this point. They are using high-power spotlights and a large crane."

Yigal: "What about the pilot?"

Shuali: "You'll soon see... oh, here it is. You see the soldiers carrying the stretcher? They are headed toward the helicopter."

Yigal: "There are more stretchers?!"

Shuali: "Wait... there, you see? Right by the chopper, being moved to the ambulances."

Yigal: "How do I run this back? I didn't count."

Shuali: "I did. Six stretchers, not including the pilot who was evacuated by the chopper."

Yigal: "And who are the others?"

Shuali: "I have no idea. Maybe Bedouin shepherds. There's a Bedouin encampment not too far from there. There they are. I got them before the sun went down. You see their tents in the background. There were quite a few of them standing around. I assume some might have gotten hurt in the crash."

Yigal: "I understand you paid the community manager of the Kibbutz a visit."

Shuali: "That's right. I wanted to know the identity of the people who were killed. I could represent their families in dealing with the insurance companies and the state."

Yigal: "And what did you find out?"

Shuali: The Kibbutznik couldn't or perhaps wouldn't disclose any further information. I decided to let it go." He smiles, "Thank God, I have plenty of cases on my desk."

7

Once Again, Ilana's Astute Eyes Peer into the Studio Camera

Ilana: "So, has the mystery been solved? Do the five unknown graves belong to Bedouins killed in an air force plane crash? And why would authorities bother to cover that up? And what happened to the person on the sixth stretcher? And also: why were the bodies buried in the cemetery of the neighboring kibbutz?

Our bold reporter Yigal went to the tents of the Sweid tribe located on the hill where the plane crashed to further investigate. We had Mr. Salah Khaldi, a reporter specializing in Arab communities join the investigation. What they found there only twisted the plot even more."

8

At the Bedouin Encampment

A spectacular view lay at the foot of the hills of the Lower Galilee. Mt. Carmel peeking over the Mediterranean and the sun setting in all its splendor. Sitting around the whispering campfire are Yigal, Salah Khaldi, the Sheikh, and a few members of the tribe. They sip bitter black coffee from small cups and snack on bitesize sweets offered by the women.

Salah: "*Kif-el-yaum ya Sheikh*... how are the herds?"

The Sheikh: "May Allah's name be blessed..."

Salah: "The wheat is tall this year... there will be much hay. New wife?" winking one eye, "Any new sons?"

The Sheikh turns his gaze to the heavens: "*Kuluh min Allah*. Allah provides. This one here," curling his moustache, the Sheikh points towards one of the women standing aside looking at the men, "we were married only a month ago... Pregnant already."

Salah: "*Shatter*, congratulations..."

The men around the fire nod their heads in congratulations, curling their mustaches. One of the youths standing above the small cups on the floor-mat pours another round of coffee.

Salah: "Do you remember when the *tayara* fell... the airplane...?"

The Sheikh: "Yes, over there, not far from just yonder," gesturing with his hand towards the growing darkness.

Salah: "The pilot was killed, along with five more people."

The Sheikh: "Yes, the pilot, Allah have mercy on his soul...? People? What people?"

Salah: "*Wallah*, I don't know."

The Sheikh: "There were lots of *jaysh*, army, we don't go near."

Yigal: "Were any of the clan harmed?"

The Sheikh: "No, by Allah's mercy, none of the *chamulah* – the clan – were hurt in the accident."

Yigal: "One of those living in the ruins, the *chirbes* there, perhaps?"

The Sheikh furrows his brow. Rubbing his eyes, massaging his face... deliberating: "Are you saying that someone may be living in the ruins?!"

Salah: "*Ana'aref*? I don't know... maybe there's some kind of foxhole there? Caves?"

The Sheikh: "By Allah, I will tell you the truth. You know how we are, sitting around the fire and the elders talk. Since I was a small child, we have always told stories of ghosts wandering the ruins of the two thousand years old village of Hosha, but I myself have... I swear," the Sheikh lays his right palm on his chest, "I have never seen anything."

Yigal: "What ghosts?"

The Sheikh: "We call them "the transparent people. *Ya'ani*... it is said that they appear on nights when the moon is full and disappear in the *wadi*... in the gorge. It is said that the *wadi* is a place of the *jinns*... a place of devils."

Yigal: "Is there anyone in the clan that has seen them recently?"

The Sheikh: "A while ago... a few days maybe... before the airplane accident, one of the girls herding the goats told her mother that she *saw*... in the *wadi*."

Yigal: "Saw what?"

The Sheikh: "*Wallah*, what can I say, there are always stories. The girl said she saw something. She was walking with the goats. She said she saw a woman, but not like one of ours. A white woman. The girl got scared and ran."

Salah: "Abu-Marwan, the television man wants to check. Perhaps there are tracks to be found. We might come at noon, tomorrow, and you would send us a youth, a tracker, which will go with us?"

The Sheikh: "*Ahalan wa-sahlan*... welcome, of course... for you, anything."

<u>9</u>

The Next Morning – on the Hill

With the help of a young Bedouin tracker, the TV crew climbs to the top of the hill. While signs of the fire are still apparent in the field, the crash site had undergone extensive work. it was obvious that diggers and loaders had turned the soil and had covered the entire area with a large number of rocks and fresh soil.

Yigal: "I wonder why they would go to so much trouble to do all of this?"

The young tracker: "Army excavators did a lot of work here and covered the crater."

Yigal: "What crater?"

Tracker: "*Tayara* made a big hole."

Salah: "He means the plane."

Tracker: "Plane make big hole in ground, but army covered up everything."

10

Back to the Program

Ilana: "Well, the five graves are not related to the Sweid tribe. It was seemingly a dead end when once again, completely by chance, we find a lead. As it turns out, in addition to the five casualties, there was a sixth person. We shall refer to him as "the sixth person" as his identity still remains unknown. What happened to the sixth person and where would he be leading us in this story? After the following commercials, we will return to our reporter, Yigal, who will navigate through the next plot twist. Stay with us.

11

At the Studio Production Lab

On the screen in front of him, Yigal plays a copy of the video Shuali taped on the day of the accident. He freezes the frame on the three ambulances evacuating the stretchers. He notices that the side of one ambulance is adorned with the words "Reuven – Ambulance Services." Yigal pulls out a large phone book, turns through the pages, and then stops on one and dials.

Receptionist: "Reuven Ambulance Services, hello?"

Yigal: "Good morning. My name is Yigal and I'm calling from Ilana Peres' TV program 'As a Matter of Fact,' would you mind if I ask you a few questions?"

Receptionist: "One moment... Reuven! Someone from the TV is asking for you."

Reuven: "What TV?!"

Receptionist: "TV?! What do I know?"

Reuven: "Hello, who is this?"

Yigal: "My name is Yigal, I'm from the TV network. I understand that you removed the wounded from the plane crash?"

Reuven: "Yes, six casualties... which show did you say?"

Yigal: "'As a Matter of Fact' with Ilana Peres. Did you

say five casualties?"

Reuven: "Not five, six. I was there. Five dead and one injured."

Yigal: "Where did you take them?"

Reuven: "Rambam hospital, Haifa. Why do you ask?"

Yigal: "The person injured was taken to Rambam?"

Reuven: "Yes. To the ER."

Yigal: "How bad was he?"

Reuven: "I don't know exactly. Broken bones, hematomas, burns... we left him there in stable condition... but after all, he was quite an old man..."

Yigal: "Do you know who he was? Or any of the deceased?"

Reuven: "No. Probably Bedouins. They were all wearing white galabias and they had white beards... still, they didn't actually look like Bedouins."

Yigal: "Why not?"

Reuven: "They seemed fair... like... European... Bedouins are darker... more tanned... know what I mean? These people were white... like they hadn't seen the light of day in a thousand years."

12

At Rambam Hospital

After receiving Yigal's report regarding his conversation with the ambulance service company, Ilana decides to visit Rambam hospital herself. She walks up to the information desk.

Ilana: "I'm here to visit the injured man from the plane crash."

Receptionist, in a flat and matter-of-fact voice: "What's his name?"

Ilana: "I don't know. An elderly man. It happened about two weeks ago, on the 21st of August."

Receptionist: Searching through her computer. A few seconds later, she raises her head: "On that day at eight o'clock in the evening they brought in an injured old man."

Ilana: "What's his name?"

Receptionist: "All it says here is 'John Doe from a crash site'"

Ilana: "Yes, that's him! Where is he?"

Receptionist: "I see that they have already transferred him to... Internal Medicine, ward C... on the third floor."

As Ilana heads towards the elevator, another receptionist from the information desk, who was listening to the conversation between Ilana and her colleague, picks up the phone and dials. She speaks into the phone, while covering her mouth with the palm of her hand.

13
At Internal Medicine Ward C

Ilana walks up to the nurses' station located in the hallway.

Ilana: "I'm looking for the old man from the plane crash accident."

Nurse, without raising her head: "Room 302, first bed on the right, by the door."

Ilana approaches the room. The bed on the right, near the door, is empty. Crumpled sheets and a blanket suggest that someone was lying there until very recently. Ilana returns to the nurses' station.

Ilana: "I was here a minute ago about the man in room 302."

Nurse, takes off her reading glasses: "Yes?"

Ilana: "He's not there!"

Nurse, with a forgiving smile: "What do you mean, he's not there?"

Ilana: "The bed is empty."

Nurse: "It's the first bed on the right."

Ilana: "Yes, that's the one I'm talking about. Maybe he's gone to use the bathroom?"

Nurse: "This patient can't go anywhere by himself. Perhaps they took him for tests." She puts here glasses back on and goes over the records. "No, I have no record of that. Are you sure you didn't go to the wrong room?" and addresses her colleague: "Shula, please show the lady to room 302."

Nurse Shula accompanies Ilana to room 302 to see for herself that the bed is indeed empty.

Shula: "Strange. I took his temperature only fifteen minutes ago."

Ilana: "Do you know who this man is? What is his name? Did you get to talk to him?"

Shula: "No. I tried but didn't get anywhere. He spoke some sort of weird language. I thought it was Arabic but the Arab nurse who works here couldn't understand him either. The patient did try to tell us something. The only person who might have understood a few words was the professor, but he couldn't really communicate with him either."

Ilana: "Professor?"

Shula: "The name of the patient lying next to him was Shmaryahu Rothman. He was released yesterday. The doctors were very respectful of him. I heard them referring to him as 'Professor.'"

Ilana: "So where is your patient?"

Shula: "This is really very strange." Shula opens the metal cabinet by the bed. "You see, his things are still here."

Ilana bends down and from the cabinet, she pulls out a long, white galabia and a wide sash. She feels something hard inside the sash. Using her fingernails, she opens the seam and pulls out a necklace with a pendant. The pendant is shaped like a goblet hanging on the chain through two rings that serve as its "handles." Ilana turns the pendant over and then back again... she closes her fist and slips the necklace into her shirt pocket.

Shula, in a panic: "Are you taking that medallion? You could get me into trouble."

Ilana, hands the nurse a card and winks: "I am an investigative TV reporter. For now, let's keep it as our little secret. Take my card. If the old man comes back or if you find out where they took him, give me a call."

As she is exiting the hospital, Ilana notices Police Captain Victor Elber, the Haifa district's chief intelligence officer. He is sitting at the canteen sipping coffee out of a paper cup. She walks over to him.

Ilana: "Good morning victor."

Victor, acting surprised: "Ilana! What a pleasant surprise. What are you doing here?"

Ilana: "Visiting."

Victor: "Family? I see. Wishing them a speedy recovery."

Ilana: "Actually, not family. I came to see the plane crash survivor, and I understand you rustled him out right under my nose. May I ask why?"

Victor: "Is this a work thing?"

Ilana: "It always is."

Victor: "What are you cooking up this time?"

Ilana: "I'm investigating the story behind the unknown individuals who were killed in the crash."

Victor: "What unknown individuals? What crash?"

Ilana: "Oh, come on Victor. I know you almost as well as your wife does. I know that you're the best detective in the north if not in the entire country, but as an actor – no offense but you're pretty mediocre, at best."

Victor finishes his drink and throws the cup in the trash can: "As an old friend and since I know that you can appreciate the gravity of this, all I can say is that the plane crash and the matter of the casualties involved is being investigated by military intelligence as well as by the police and the secret service. I can't divulge anything else at this point. If you handle this information responsibly, which I'm sure you will, I promise to personally update you with any further information that can be made known to the public."

Victor taps his hand to his forehead in a semi-salute, says "Goodbye" and walks away.

14

The CEO of the TV Channel has Summoned the Director of Programming for an Unusual Conversation

Obviously, Ilana's visit to the hospital touched a sensitive nerve. Less than three hours later, Ilan Yaffe, the director of programming, receives a phone call from the CEO. Ilan calls Ilana immediately after the unusual conversation ends.

Ilan: "The CEO of the channel spoke to me personally. He asked if we have been looking into a plane crash in the north. The truth is that I didn't know how to answer."
Ilana: "And what did he say about it?"
Ilan: "Very simple, he told me to order you to drop it."

Ilana: "Oh come on! You're not serious."

Ilan: "I am."

Ilana: "For what reason?"

Ilan: "For the reasons that the matter of the plane crash is part of a very delicate investigation that we don't want to disrupt."

Ilana: "And what are you telling me?"

Ilan, with the hint of a smile: "I'm telling you that you are probably onto something interesting and that you should keep digging, but be very careful."

Ilana: "You mean, keep a low profile?"

Ilan: "I admire your profile, but yeah, be cautious, at least until things are clearer."

After the visit to the Rambam Hospital, where Ilana met Inspector Victor Elbar, the northern district's chief intelligence officer, Ilana had thought of slowing down a bit, but a phone call she received the next morning disrupted – or perhaps, further advanced her plans.

<u>15</u>

An Unexpected Phone Call

The next day following her visit to the hospital; Ilana is sitting at her busy desk, looking for a spot for her coffee mug when the phone rings. It is Shula, the nurse, speaking hesitantly.

Shula: "Erm... Hello... Ilana?... I'm the nurse... You left me your business card... at Rambam."

Ilana: "Yes, Shula, is that you? Good afternoon."

Shula: "You asked me about the old man who was lying in 302 by the door... so one of the orderlies told me that a few minutes before you arrived, he was instructed to immediately take the patient back to the emergency room. While he was there, he saw the patient being wheeled out to an ambulance. I don't know if I should be telling you this, but it all feels very wrong to me... so there you have it..."

A hushed moment passes and before Ilana manages to respond, the call hangs up.

Ilana calls Yigal to her office.

Ilana: "It turns out that the mysterious old man who survived the accident was smuggled out and taken elsewhere right under my nose. He may even have died. Apparently, it happened right when I was on my way up from the reception desk to the third floor. Someone warned someone that I was coming. I don't know why, but that someone really didn't want me to see this person.

Nevertheless, the visit was not entirely in vain. I learned that right next to his bed, lay a man by the name of Shmaryahu Rothman, whom the nurse referred to as the 'Professor'. I checked to see if such a person actually exists and indeed, he's not just any professor, he is an Israel Prize laureate, a famous, albeit controversial, archaeologist, a professor of theology, and an expert in Eastern old languages. Please make contact and meet with him."

16

Shmarhayu Rothman

Yigal and his TV crew head to Denia neighborhood atop Mt. Carmel to meet Professor Shmaryahu in his modest home. Leah, the professor's wife greets them at the door while the professor is seated in the living room in his pajamas.

Leah: "Please keep it short, the professor has just come out of the hospital."

Shmaryahu: "It's alright. Come in. Please sit down. My dear, perhaps we could offer our guests a cold drink?"

Yigal: "I really don't want to impose. Just a few questions if I may…"

Shmaryahu, carefully examining the cameraman and soundman holding the boom. "Which program is this for?"

Yigal: "Ilana Peres' As a Matter of Fact."

Shmaryahu: "Ilana Peres. Well, that is alright then. For a moment I was worried you are from one of those reality shows…"

Yigal: "I understand you were admitted to Rambam hospital?"

Shmaryahu: "Yes, what can I say, at my age, the machine doesn't run as smoothly as it used to. From time to time, one needs to visit the body shop… ha ha…"

With his heavy German accent, the professor seemed to be entertained by his own humor.

Yigal: "There was an old man in the bed next to you who was speaking a language no one could understand."

Shmaryahu: "Oh, yes. He was very confused… did not really talk, only mumbled a few words here and there.

What was interesting is that he mixed Aramaic, biblical Hebrew, and a little bit of Arabic... but he was really very jumbled."

Yigal: "Could you make anything out of what he was saying?"

Shmaryahu: "The thing is, I had just undergone surgery. The plumbing was a little bit clogged if you know what I mean, so my plumbing needed an overhaul... ha... I was on painkillers. You might say that I too was in a bit of a daze."

Yigal: "And what did you manage to understand?"

Shmaryahu: "He spoke... he kept mentioning a goblet. Kept saying in Aramaic 'Kubayat'... yes, he repeated that word many times. Something about a goblet that needs to be protected. One might suggest that he was obsessed with that."

Yigal: "I'd like to show you something. Please look here." Yigal turns his smartphone toward the professor.

Shmaryahu: "Oh, where did you take that picture?"

Yigal: "This pendant was hidden in the old man's sash."

Shmaryahu: "Really? That is very interesting. I would like to see that medallion."

Yigal: "Why? What is so special about it?"

Leah places a tray on the glass table, walks over to her husband, and covers his lap with the wool blanket that had fallen to the floor. "Please have a drink. I hope you are almost done. The professor must get some rest."

The Professor makes no effort to hide his obvious annoyance: "It is alright dear... It's alright."

Shmaryahu: "It would be interesting to date this object. You know? These days one can scientifically prove the age of things."

Yigal: "Can you give an estimate?"

Shmaryahu: "I would not be surprised if it is extremely ancient. A few hundred years, who knows, perhaps even more."

Yigal: "If we manage to bring the pendant to you, would it give you any more clues as to the old man's identity?"

Shmaryahu: "A clue? Oh, yes... a clue. Perhaps even more than just a clue. If it is what I think it is, this pendant could open an entire box of clues... a Pandora's Box... ha."

<u>17</u>

In the Lab at the Technion

Following Shmaryhau's recommendation, an appointment is made for Yigal to meet Dr. Yaacov Ernan the very next day at the Technion Institute's Isotope research laboratory.

Yigal: "I'm Yigal... from Channel One... we spoke on the phone."

Dr. Ernan: "Yes, you wanted to examine the age of an artifact?"

Yigal, pulls the chain with the medallion out of his pocket. "Yes, we would like to know the age of this pendant."

Dr. Ernan: "It may take a few days. It also costs money."

Yigal: "I'm probably right guessing that a few more days means nothing to an object such as this."

Dr. Ernan: "Strange. It looks like a chalice."

Yigal: "Right. But why is that so strange?"

Dr. Ernan: "It is the second goblet I would have tested these past few days."

Yigal, astonished: "Someone else brought you a medallion like this?"

Dr. Ernan: "No... not quite... never mind... come back in three days. Call me just in case."

18

Morning Meeting at the Studio

Ilana: "Dr. Ernan's comment about the 'second grail' left you with a few questions, right?"

Yigal: "Of course, but as you could see, the doc wasn't happy, to say the least, to respond to direct questions about that. What mattered to me at that moment was for him to check the pendant that I had brought. From my experience, if I may paraphrase Ecclesiastes, there's a time to ask, and a time for every answer."

Ilana: "A question mark left on the table in the first act will appear as an exclamation point in the third?"

Yigal: "Yeah, something like that."

Ilana: "Did you get the results."

Yigal: "Three days later."

Ilana: "I'm dying to hear... but I understand you took the findings to Professor Shmaryahu."

19
_____

Once Again, at Shmaryahu Rothman's Place

Yigal and his crew set out toward the Professor's house once again. Upon their arrival, they find him pruning the roses in his garden.

Yigal: "Good Morning."

Shmaryahu: "Oh... Welcome, welcome. Come sit..."

They sit in the white plastic chairs set out on the grass.

Shmaryahu: "I apologize for not offering you anything. My wife is out on her favorite pastime – shopping... ha... ha"

Yigal: "It's okay."

Shmaryahu, with a smile and a wink, "We have about half an hour of quiet until my wife is back. Have you brought the medallion?"

Yigal sets the medallion on the table. Shmaryahu pulls a Swiss Army Knife with a magnifying glass out of his brown corduroy pants. Lifting the medallion, he examines it.

Shmaryahu: "Did you see the inscription?"

Yigal, leans forward, straining his eyes: "Yes. There is something engraved here."

Shmaryahu: "Jesus Nazarenus, Jesus of Nazareth."

Yigal: "And what does that mean?"

Shmaryahu: "It is too soon to know, nevertheless I do have my guesses. I am curious as to the age of this artifact."

Yigal: takes the lab report out of his pocket and hands it to the professor: "These are the results from the tests conducted at the Technion's Isotope Department laboratory."

Shmaryahu, looking at the document. "Intriguing... fascinating. Carbon dating... Such tests have exceptionally accurate results. As you can see, the chain and the pendant are not of the same age. It is as I originally thought. The chain is merely decades old, but the medallion... hand-made... Truly an antique... an extremely rare object. It is about two thousand years old!"

Yigal: "And how would such an antique fall into the hands of a Bedouin?"

Shmaryahu: "Not a Bedouin!"

Yigal, widening his eyes: "But???"

Shmaryahu: "I can only guess that the old man in the hospital bed beside me is a member of the Order of the Grail Keepers."

Yigal: "The Keepers of the Grail?!"

Shmaryahu: "That's right. The Holy Grail is one of the most important symbols in Christianity. It was lost the day that Jesus was arrested at Gethsemane. According to some beliefs, the Grail was brought to England. The Knights of the Round Table, led by Sir Percival, set out to find it. They hoped that if King Arthur could drink from the Grail, he would be cured, and recover from his sickness. Other traditions hold that one of the Apostles brought the Grail to Montserrat Abbey in Spain. It might sound like fiction, but Himmler, Hitler's lieutenant, organized a team of German scientists that searched for it there. He believed that finding the Grail would grant the Nazis superpowers that none could challenge."

Yigal: "And who are the people in this Order of the Grail?"

Shmaryahu: "Do you know where the crash in which the old man was hurt occurred?"

Yigal: "On one of the hills east of route 70. The road between Yagur interchange and Shfaram."

Shmaryahu, slaps his palm on his forehead: "Of course... now it all makes sense..."

Yigal, each sentence coming out of the Professor's mouth sounds to him like a riddle: "What makes sense?"

Shmaryahu: "Yes, this old man muttered gibberish and half sentences. He kept repeating the word "Hosha." I thought he was trying to say his name: 'Hoshea.' Now, I understand he was referring to a place. 'Hosha,' an

Arab village built on the ruins of Usha from the days of the *tannaim* sages. For a while, after the Bar-Kochba rebellion, it was the seat of the grand *Sanhedrin*."

Yigal: "And you think that the old man lived there, within the ruins?"

Shmaryahu: "No...no... not within the ruins."

Yigal: "But?"

Shmaryahu: "Beneath the ruins. We already know that Hosha – Usha hill rests atop caves and tunnels. I believe that the old man and his clan lived there... with their treasure.

Yigal: "The Grail?"

Shmaryahu: "Right. The members of the 'Order' swore to guard the Grail until the return of the one who drank from it last."

Yigal: "Jesus?"

Shmaryahu: "Jesus Christ, himself and none other."

Yigal: Are you saying they have been living there, underground, for two thousand years?"

Shmaryahu: "NO, not exactly. There is no need to get carried away. I suppose... In fact, we do have historical evidence that they lived alongside their Arab neighbors. The French historian Champollion, who journeyed alongside Emperor Napoleon during his jaunt in the Holy Land, tells of a Jewish/Christian family whom he met in Hosha, where the emperor stayed on his way to the fortified city of Acre."

"Champollion writes that he saw a writ of protection granted to them by Saladin. According to what he was told, an officer of the Crusaders whose capital was Acre – kidnapped one of the clan's girls. The young girl escaped the night before the battle of Hattin and was caught by a Muslim patrol. She gave the Muslim general valuable information about the poor state of the crusader army. The following day, Saladin defeated the Crusaders at the famous Hattin battle and ended the Crusader presence in the Holy Land. As a token of appreciation, Saladin granted the clan a writ of protection."

Yigal: "And they've lived there since?"

Shmaryahu: "Probably. We also know about a family in Peki'in, which has lived there since the days of the Second Temple, and there are surely other families that did not go into exile. I presume that in 1948, when the Carmeli Brigade took over the Arab village and its residents fled to Lebanon, the family went back into hiding under the ground."

Yigal: "And you think that they have been living there to this day? "

Shmaryahu: "It is a bit of a wild guess, though not completely unlikely. Technically, it is possible. We know of people who have lived in caves and tunnels such as these for an extended period of time. They definitely do not lack water and can subsist on dried fruit such as figs, raisins, carobs, and so forth – just like our very own Rabbi Shimon Bar-Yochai hiding in a cave from the Romans. It is completely possible that they would occasionally go out and return to the caves."

Yigal: "Maybe this is the source of the Bedouin legends of the "Transparent People."

Shmaryahu: "It could be that the crashed plane collapsed the ceiling of the cave."

Yigal: "The Bedouins said that the army filled in a large crater that formed as a result of the crash."

Shmaryahu: "The important question is what befell the Grail. I have no doubt that rescue digs should be conducted onsite. Think about it: what if the Holy Grail really is buried there? It could be a global sensation. A huge earthquake. The whole Christian world would be on its feet. It would be the most important archaeological find of the past few centuries. Something on the scale of the discovery of the Dead Sea Scrolls... or the tomb of Tutankhamun..."

At that moment Leah, Shmaryahu's wife, arrives and parks her car in front of the house.

Shmaryahu: "The health watchdog has arrived. From now on, not one word about the Grail."

Leah exits the car, holding plastic bags filled with various purchases.

Leah: "Hello. I see my husband has become a celebrity. You must excuse us. The Professor needs to take his medicine now."

Yigal: "Of course."

He stands and picks up the medallion from the table, "Goodbye Professor, and thank you."

Shmaryahu, whispering: "We will keep in touch."

20

At the Studio, Ilana Recaps

Ilana: "So, this is what we know so far... a plane crash, five mysterious graves, one injured elderly man who has since disappeared, 'transparent people' and now, the "Holy Grail" from which Jesus and his disciples drank at the "Last Supper." The grail, the entire Christian world has been searching for, for two thousand years. The chalice that is awaiting Jesus' resurrection, buried perhaps under 'Mishnah' old Usha, not too far from the Church of the Annunciation in Nazareth, where Jesus' mother Mary found out she was with child."

"You must admit that here is a story fit for 'Indiana Jones', and as you will soon see, we haven't yet touched the tip of this incredible chain of events. With the help of Israel Prize laureate and renowned archeologist, Shmaryahu Rothman, we have managed to secure the National Antiques Department permit to dig up the crater that was formed by the crash and covered over by the Army."

21
Digging Hoshea Hill

A backhoe and a handful of people holding shovels are digging where the military covered the crater that was formed due to the crash. Shmaryahu, wearing a Pith Helmet and safari apparel is sitting on a folding chair under a parasol. Yigal and his team are busy filming. Suddenly, one of the workers yells from the bottom of the pit.

Worker: "There's an opening here."

Shmaryahu and Yigal leap toward the edge of the pit. Indeed, a dark, one-meter diameter opening is revealed.

Yigal: "I'm going down there together with the cameraman."

Shmaryahu: "I am going down there with you."

Yigal: "Absolutely out of the question. I promised your

wife that we are going to the studio to record a brief interview."

Shmaryahu: "I can decide for myself."

Yigal, smiling wide: "Are you sure?"

Shmaryahu, yields: "Fine. I will wait for you here. But don't leave me hanging too long."

Yigal and the cameraman, equipped with a small video camera, vanish into the opening in the wall of the pit. The light on the camera helps them to see that they are in a relatively large room with nooks in its walls. On one side of the room, there is a "window" facing east to the tall cliff hanging over the wadi. The rock wall opens onto some sort of balcony covered by a thick bush. In the "room," shattered rock and aluminum debris are noticeable. Yigal picks up scraps of bandages, empty infusion bags, bloody gauze pads, and rubber gloves, from the floor.

22

Meanwhile, Outside

Meanwhile, outside, two military command-cars are coming up the hill. A squad of soldiers jumps out and encircles the pit. An officer approaches Shmaryahu.

Officer: "Can you tell me what you're doing here?"

Shmaryahu: "I am Shmaryahu Rothman... Professor of archeology and Israel Prize laureate."

Officer: "And who gave you permission to dig here?"

Shmaryahu, pulls out from his pocket the permit he received: "I have a license issued by the Antiquities Department."

Officer: "You must leave at once!"

Shmaryahu: "Did you read the permit?"

Officer, folds the permit and hands it back to Shmaryahu: "I declare it a closed military area. We will notify the directory of the Antiques Department accordingly."

23
Yigal and the Cameraman are Walking Around in the Cave

They discover an underground spring, stone bunks, rags, and large ceramic vessels containing carobs and dried figs... the flash of the camera begins to dim.

Cameraman: "My batteries are about to run out. I suggest we go back."

Yigal: "Just a minute."

Cameraman: "We must leave now. We can come back with proper gear."

They head to the cave opening. The cameraman is the first to stick his head out. He sees the two fully armed soldiers standing over the top of the pit and immediately recoils.

Cameraman, whispering: "There are soldiers out there."
Yigal: "Quick, change the tapes"
Cameraman: "I have another tape which I recorded before, on the top of the hill."
Yigal: "That's good. Stick that one in."
The cameraman switches the tapes. Yigal grabs the tape they recorded in the cave and shoves it into his underwear.

24

Two Weeks Later, the Follow-Up Program Airs on TV

After the program's theme accompanied by dramatic music fit for the gravity of the subject, Ilana delivers her opening words with a serious demeanor.

Ilana: "After we aired the first episode of this story, we were flooded with an unprecedented number of inquiries. People literally called from all over the world. We had no idea how much the legend of the Holy Grail, or maybe it is no longer a legend – still resonates in the hearts of millions, some two thousand years after it disappeared. Our valiant investigator, Yigal, went down to the Caves of Hosha, aka Ancient Usha, searching for the transparent people and the Holy Grail."

Yigal: "Naturally, we were detained by soldiers. But all in all, they treated us well."

Ilana: "And what did you find in the cave?"

Yigal: "As the footage shows, we found clear evidence that people were living there underground. We shall refer to them as the 'Transparent People.' We discovered an elaborate system that allowed for living conditions, of cavemen that is. We found the remnants of bandages and medical equipment that suggest that the soldiers of Unit 669 treated a number of injured after the roof of the cave collapsed."

Ilana:" And what didn't you find?"

Yigal: "We did not find a Grail!" Yigal smiles as if he were offering an apology.

Ilana: "So, have we reached a dead end once again?"

Yigal: "Not quite."

Ilana: "I understand that a day after our last episode, you received a strange phone call?!"

Yigal: "Correct."

Ilana: "What did the anonymous caller tell you?"

Yigal: "He said that he knows what I was looking for and that he could help me."

Ilana: "So you made arrangements to meet?"

Yigal: "Indeed."

Ilana: "At the request of the caller, we recorded the meeting concealing his face and distorting his voice. For our purposes, we shall call him Itzik. His real name will remain under wraps.

25

In the Studio, Yigal Interviews Itzik Who is Sitting with His Back to the Camera

Yigal: "Good evening, Itzik."

Itzik: "Good evening."

Yigal: "You called me a few days ago saying you can help me with something I am looking for."

Itzik: "Correct."

Yigal: "You've asked to remain anonymous. Why is that? Are you afraid of something? Or perhaps, someone?"

Itzik: "I am not afraid of anyone, but my privacy is important to me."

Yigal: "You did say it would be okay for me to mention that you serve in a special unit as part of your reserve duty."

Itzik: "True."

Yigal: "A unit that specializes in search and rescue efforts. I understand you were part of the team that was sent to the site of the plane crash near Shfaram junction. Tell us about it."

Itzik: "The team was on call. We were flown from our home base to the scene by helicopter."

Yigal: "And what did you see?"

Itzik: "The plane had crashed head-on right into the hill. There was some sort of subterranean cave, and the plane just drilled its way in with its nose. I would say that about a third of the plane, including the cockpit, was stuck in the ground. We managed to manipulate our way down under the ground, somehow."

Yigal: "And what did you see down there?"

Itzik: "It was a very dark cave. We had to use our flashlights. Not long after, they brought in army cranes and projectors. We found the pilot."

Yigal: "Was he dead?"

Itzik: "Yes. He didn't stand a chance."

Yigal: "What else did you find in the cave?"

Itzik: "To our surprise, we found six more individuals. At first only four, and then two more. It was quite a surprise because we weren't warned that there might be people down there."

Yigal: "And what was their condition?"

Itzik: "Four were dead. Two injured. We administrated emergency treatment, one died despite our efforts. The other, as far as I know, was later taken by ambulance to Rambam hospital."

Yigal: "So what did you do next?"

Itzik: "There wasn't much we could do. Since the plane blocked the entire top of the tunnel, we couldn't evacuate anyone at first. We only got them out after the crane pulled out the wreckage of the plane."

Yigal: "Who did you think those people were?"

Itzik: "The truth is that I didn't know then and I still don't. They looked a bit strange."

Yigal: "What do you mean 'strange'"?

Itzik: "They were wearing these long white galabias. They had long white beards. Long white hair. It was so dark in there that I could only see them by using a flashlight. Our medic shined his flashlight directly into one of the men's eyes. They were completely white. Like, not just the eyeball but the pupil as well. I got the chills when I saw that."

Yigal: "Did you want to tell me anything about the chalice?"

Itzik: "Yeah, so one of the men was holding it. I mean like really held it close to his heart with both hands, and he was already dead. One of the guys tried to get it out of his grip but couldn't."

Yigal: "And then what happened?"

Itzik: "After the debris was cleared away, they lowered a ladder, and more people went down there. Officers, medical personnel, and soldiers from the military's Rabbinical services who deal with evacuating the fallen. I don't want to get too graphic, but one of the men who got killed was scattered all over the place. The Rabbinical servicemen dealt with that."

Yigal: "Did anyone do anything with the goblet?"

Itzik: "I didn't notice. It was only when we were outside that I saw the bodies before they were zipped up in body bags. They were laid side by side. I saw that the man who was holding the goblet didn't have it anymore. His hands were on his chest as before, but without the goblet."

Yigal: "Did that seem curious to you?"

Itzik: "Not really. On the contrary, it seemed perfectly normal that someone would have taken it out of his hands. I thought nothing of it."

Yigal: "And do you have any idea as to who might have taken the goblet?"

Itzik: "Not at all. It seemed like a simple chalice. It reminded me of the trophies they give out at sporting events. I really didn't read too much into it. I totally forgot about it until I watched your program. It was only then that I realized the goblet might be something significant."

Yigal: "And that is why you decided to contact me?"

Itzik: "That's right."

Yigal: "Don't get me wrong, but your testimony regarding the goblet is far more important than what you can imagine. Is there anyone else who can corroborate what you have described?"

Itzik, pauses with apprehension before he responds: "Yes, there might be."

Yigal: "Can you provide me with their details?"

Itzik, pulls a cell phone out of his jacket pocket and shows Yigal the screen. "Here. Look."

Yigal: "I must have a copy of this photo."

Itzik: "Give me your number and I will forward it to you... on one condition..."

Yigal: "What would that be?"

Itzik: "That that would be it, and nothing more to do with me."

Yigal: "Fair enough. Thank you so much for agreeing to this interview. I promise you won't hear from me again.

26
At the Knesset, Jerusalem

The bright mid-morning sun washes the plaza outside the entrance to the Knesset Parliament building in Jerusalem. Ilana and her team approach the entrance to the rectangular building.

Ilana: "It turns out that despite their busy schedules, our legislators watch our program or have at least heard of it. This week, MK Zeev Levi from the "Torah Unity" party addressed it during Question Time. We have come here to hear the government's response."

The assembly hall is almost empty. From a tall podium, the Speaker of the Knesset oversees the procedures with a bored demeanor.

The Speaker: "Question number 1327, presented by MK Zeev Levi from the Torah Unity party. If you please Sir."

MK Zeev, with his long black beard over his chest and wearing a black Yarmulka, steps up to the microphone stationed in the aisle. "Last week, as part of the TV show 'As A Matter of Fact,' there was an item..."

Bored MK, one of the only MKs present hisses from his seat: "I had no idea that 'Torah Unity' MKs watch sinful tv shows..."

MK Zeev, responds jokingly: "And I had no idea that my esteemed colleague here is such an expert on Jewish Law..."

The Speaker: "MK Zeev, please continue."

MK Zeev: "I was just responding to my friend."

The Speaker: "I gave you the floor to ask, not to respond. I am asking the present members not to interfere..."

MK Zeev: "My question is brief and simple: is it true that the object, some refer to as 'The Holy Grail', was indeed found in the ruins of ancient Usha?"

The Speaker: "Let's see who the respondent... I see the respondent is the honorable Minister Haim Limon. If you please, Sir..."

Minister Haim Limon, steps up to the podium and reads out of a sheet of paper in a monotone voice: "In response to Question number 1237, the government has no knowledge pertaining to what is referred to as 'The Holy Grail' that was mentioned in the TV program 'As A Matter of Fact.'" The minister folds the paper and turns to walk off the stand.

MK Zeev: "I wish to respond, if I may."

The Speaker, turns to the minister who has since stepped off the stand: "If you please, sir, one moment please."

The Speaker, addresses MK Zeev: "Yes, please ask your follow-up question..."

MK Zeev: "Has the government or the Ministry of Religious Services received an official petition from anyone?"

The Speaker: "MK Zeev Levi, I believe that the minister would have a hard time responding to such a general question, could you be more specific as to whom 'anyone' might refer to?"

MK Zeev: "I will be more specific. Has the government received a request, either through the Prime Minister's Office or the Ministries of Foreign Affairs or Religious Affairs, from the Vatican, regarding the Holy Grail and how does the government intend to respond to the request?"

Minister Limon: "I do not know. The offices you mentioned receive dozens of inquiries and requests every day on a wide variety of matters."

MK Zeev: "Mr. Speaker, the honorable minister seems to be avoiding the question."

The Speaker: "The Minister will look into it. We will recess now and reconvene at ten o'clock sharp to resume today's agenda." The Speaker taps the gavel and declares: "This meeting is adjourned."

27

In one of the Knesset Hallways, Ilana Walks Up to MK Zeev Levi

Ilana: "MK Levi, good morning."

MK Zeev, with a welcoming face: "A blessed morning to you too."

Ilana: "Do you really know something about the Vatican reaching out to the government regarding the Holy Grail?"

MK Zeev: "I have reason to believe they have."

Ilana: "Do you know the nature of their query?"

MK Zeev: "To my knowledge, the Vatican is demanding to receive the Grail if it has indeed been found."

Ilana: "And if it really does exist, would you object to its being handed to the Vatican?"

MK Zeev: "Of course!!!"

Ilana: "Why is that?"

MK Zeev: "Too many treasures were pillaged by the Romans and taken to Rome. If indeed a goblet from the days of the Second Temple was found in Usha, it would belong to the Jewish people and should be rightfully kept in the Israel Museum in Jerusalem."

Ilana: "You would agree to have the chalice Jesus drank from on display at the Israel Museum?"

MK Zeev, smiles widely: "If indeed Jesus' fingerprints will be found on the goblet, we will agree to have the President of the State of Israel himself deliver it as a special gift to the Pope."

Ilana: "And if they won't find fingerprints and decide anyway to surrender the goblet, will you view that as reason for a coalition parliamentary crisis?"

MK Zeev, smiling diplomatically: "You journalists always look for crisis... but I will be straight with you. We do not see this as something to sneeze at – we know exactly what kind of a storm such a thing can potentially cause in the Christian world and what past memories it can evoke. We really don't need that right now."

Ilana: "And if..."

MK Zeev: "You know what our regular answer is ..."

Ilana: "You'll go by what the 'High Council of the Torah Sages' instructs you to do?"

MK Zeev, straightens his beard smiling: "You took the words right out of my mouth."

28

Gethsemane, East of the Old City Walls

Ilana: "After our short visit to the Knesset, we decided to head to Gethsemane where, according to the New Testament, Jesus was arrested. Well, this is where it happened. Some two thousand years ago. Perhaps it was under that tree over here, by this large rock."

29

The Old City, Jerusalem

A full moon hangs over the domes and minarets. The ringing of church bells mingles with the prayers of the muezzins emerging from the mosques. A number of shadows pass through a narrow and dark alley, heavy-bearded men wearing long black coats. They slip through a small wooden door into one of the old, low-slung houses. Inside, a narrow basement, lit by a faint yellowish gloom emanating from a bare lamp fixed onto the ceiling.

Sitting hunched around a heavy wooden table are a handful of bearded men, members of "The committee for the Defense Against False Messianism." The light from above hones their features and casts thick shadows over the table.

MK Zeev – Head of the committee: "Gentlemen, I have called for this urgent meeting, and I thank you all for coming on such short notice. I shall get right to it: A few days ago, we found out about an interesting development, quite unique which could have considerable ramifications for our actions against the growing false Messianic claims."

The rabbis listen attentively and quietly. Their wide-brimmed hats still shading their faces.

MK Zeev, continues in his low voice: "You must have heard of the Grail, as it is called, by those who believe that he and his followers drank from in their last supper. And here," he raises his voice, "in these past few days, that artifact may have been found, right here in the Holy Land."

One of the Rabbis: "And why is this news? These cups have already turned up in the past and they were all tested and found to be counterfeits, so why is this any different?"

MK Zeev: "It is quite possible and even probable that the honorable rabbi is right. The difference this time is that it is here in the Land of Israel. Of course, it will be found to be false. Nevertheless, the mere presentation of this artifact could cause a great noise and controversy."

One of the Rabbis: "And what are you suggesting, Sir?"

MK Zeev: "The discovery of the Grail would drive a mass awakening and will resurface sleeping conflicts. I am of the opinion that we must do everything God enables us in order to quash this wave before it rises. Send the genie back into the goblet, so to speak."

Rabbi Arieh: "If I may... I am of the opinion we should consider this matter very carefully. I myself do not believe in the legend of the Grail, of course. However, if indeed as the distinguished chairman pointed out, there might be a chance of the item being revealed, any attempt to make it disappear will surely fail.

I am not so certain that in this era, the discovery of the Grail will evoke such a tremendous reaction.

If anything, rumors of Jews trying to sabotage such a revelation could bring about greater anger and insult. It might be best to expose the fact it exists, and after tests that would surely refute its authenticity, it will be quickly forgotten. It would be better to disprove it rather than create a new myth."

Chairman: "I thank Rabbi Arieh for his words. We are all familiar with our colleague Rabbi Arieh's eloquent way of presenting the reverse argument. With that said, I am adamant we do what we can to prevent the exposure of this thing."

Consenting murmurs are heard across the table.

MK Zeev: "I see that you all agree to grant me the power to act with the utmost determination against this. I shall update the committee with any development. Thank you once again for answering my urgent call to convene today."

30

The Intercontinental Hotel, Jerusalem

Night. The view of the old city from the Intercontinental Hotel is spectacular. By day, the hotel plaza buzzes with tourists and vendors, but now, at midnight, only one person leans forward against the cold iron railing.

Suddenly a long shadow is cast on the stone pavement. Footsteps can be heard. The leaning man straightens his back and turns on his heels to greet the person he was been waiting for. Out of the darkness emerges a tall black hat. A long, dark coat. A countenance crowned by a bushy red beard shines through the dim light of the streetlamp. He approaches the waiting man. Standing close to one another, they speak in quiet tones. The man who had been waiting reaches deep into his coat and hands the red-bearded man a hefty envelope. The red-bearded man takes the envelope, puts it in his coat pocket, walks away, and is immediately engulfed in darkness, his long shadow following him.

31

At the Studio, Ilana and Yigal Continue to Examine What is Known Thus Far

Ilana: "Let's recap. As of now, it looks like we have managed to collect a lot of information and yet, we haven't gotten anywhere."

Yigal: "That's right. The only evidence we have concerning the Grail is the testimony of a Unit 669 reservist who claims he had seen it clutched in the hands of one of the men who died in the plane crash. Who took it out of the dead man's hands? And what did they do with it? That is probably the key to finding out the chain of events."

Ilana: "And let's not forget the comment made by Dr. Ernan from the Technion isotope laboratory about the 'second goblet.'"

Yigal: "Right. Though Dr. Ernan refuses to elaborate, and it isn't quite clear to which goblet he was referring.

Ilana: "Well, we can ask the right questions, but do we have any answers?"

Yigal:" We've composed a list of everyone we know who was there at the time of the crash. Military and police personnel, fire fighters, Air Force, medical staff as well as the Military's Rabbinical services specialists – who were busy gathering the remains of the dead, which is why we decided to focus on them. It is a small unit under the Northern Command consisting of a Rabbi and three sergeants. It took many efforts and thanks to the IDF Spokesperson's Unit, we managed to get permission to interview Rabbi Yehuda Amar."

32

Rabbi Yehuda Amar Meets Yigal at his Office at the Northern Command Base

Yigal: "Thank you for agreeing to do this interview, sir."

Rabbi Amar: "My pleasure. How can I help?"

Yigal: "Do you remember the plane crash?"

Rabbi Amar: "I do, unfortunately."

Yigal: "Can you describe your role in that incident?"

Rabbi Amar: "We usually get called to assist in disastrous situations in which, sadly, people get hurt. Our people are also trained to help the medical teams if needed but mainly, our job is to protect the honor of our fallen soldiers."

Yigal: "Kind of like the 'Zaka' search and rescue organization?"

Rabbi Amar: "You could say that, yes. Zaka operates where there are terror attacks and accidents involving mostly civilians. We get called in to handle incidents concerning military personnel, in times of peace and certainly in times of war."

Yigal: "What do you remember from the plane incident?"

Rabbi Amar: "It so happens I was off that day. I got a call at home from the Northern Command's Operations desk. I arrived on the scene in my car, about an hour or a little bit more after it happened. The rest of the team came more or less when I did, some even sooner."

Yigal: "And what did you find?"

Rabbi Amar: "If I remember correctly, there were six or seven fatalities. The pilot and a number of civilians."

Yigal: "Who were the civilians?"

Rabbi Amar: "We didn't identify them there. They were taken to the hospital."

Yigal: "Excuse me for getting a bit graphic, but who is responsible for putting the fatalities into the plastic body bags?"

Rabbi Amar: "Yes, that is indeed a tough job. Usually, it is I, or one of my men, who gives the OK to zip up the bags, once we've checked the bodies. If we find body parts that we can match for certain with a particular body, we do the best we can to collect and pack them in the same body bag on the spot, to avoid any mishaps later."

Yigal: "Do you know of a certain object that was attached to one of the bodies? The civilians that is?"

Rabbi Amar: "I'm not aware of anything in particular. We don't deal with those things at that stage. If you mean wedding rings, necklaces, watches, and such – those things are collected at a later stage and then given to the families of the deceased."

Yigal: "The soldiers said that one of the deceased was holding a goblet."

Rabbi Amar: "A goblet?!"

Yigal: "Like a chalice... not large, possibly made of copper, clasped in the hands of one of the civilian fatalities. Did you see an object like that?"

Rabbi Amar: "As I said, I only arrived toward the end of it all. The bodies were still on site, but they were already in the bags, so even if there was anything I wouldn't have seen it at that point."

Yigal: "There are testimonies that there a goblet there. Is it possible that one of your soldiers took it?"

Rabbi Amar: "Do you have evidence of such a thing?"

Yigal: "No, I'm simply suggesting what might have happened."

Rabbi Amar: "No, I have no knowledge of that happening and it doesn't sound reasonable to me."

Yigal: "Could you check?"

Rabbi Amar: "Of course. Is there a reason you are so interested in this object?"

Yigal: "Have you ever heard of the Holy Grail?"

Rabbi Amar: "What do you mean?"

Yigal: "The goblet that Jesus and his disciples drank from at the Last Supper as described in the New Testament."

Rabbi Amar: "Ah... that Grail... no, I am not well versed in these matters."

Yigal: "This is no more than a theory, but is it possible that there may be a link between the Christian tradition and the civilians killed in the plane crash?"

Rabbi Amar, strokes his beard and after a brief pause, says: "I heard later that they probably weren't Jewish... but I didn't go into it."

Yigal: "Thank you for your time, Sir."

Yigal and the Rabbi shake hands and bid each other farewell.

33

The Technion Institute, Haifa

Nighttime. The parking lot in front of the laboratory building at the Technion Institute is faintly illuminated by two lights standing posted in two of its corners. The burnt-out bulbs in the other two have not yet been replaced. It's eleven o'clock at night. There's only one car parked there, caught in the headlights of another car that is slowly gliding into the parking lot. The approaching car comes to a stop. Its headlights shut off. The door opens and a tall man with a thick red beard hanging over the upright collar of his long coat steps out of the car.

The man stands for a moment and looks at the front of the building. All the floors are dark, except for a few windows on the fourth floor from which a faint yellowish light emanates. The man approaches the front door. It is locked. He returns to his car and takes a long crowbar out of the trunk. He uses it to force open the door and goes into the building. He shines a flashlight on the sign behind the darkened reception desk. The beam of the flashlight focuses on a row of silver aluminum letters: " Genetics Laboratory – Fourth Floor." The man uses his flashlight to light his way and climbs up the staircase to the fourth floor.

In the genetics laboratory, Dr. Salim Jubran is busy performing various tests. A particularly urgent and intriguing matter has made the doctor stay in the laboratory this late by himself. The Doctor is tearing off data printouts coming from the computer. He inspects them while rubbing his eyes in bewilderment, muttering to himself: "Unbelievable... absolutely incredible..."

Red Beard arrives at the door of the laboratory. He lightly presses down on the handle. The door opens. He leans the crowbar against the wall by the door and enters. The surprised Dr. Jubran lifts his eyes from the paper printout in his hands with great astonishment.

Dr. Jubran: "Who are you? How did you get in here? What are you doing here?"
Red Beard: "Where is the Grail?"
Dr. Jubran: "There's no Grail here. Please leave right now!"

The bearded man ignores Dr. Jubran's demands and starts snooping around. He abruptly opens drawers and cupboards, knocking over glassware that shatters on the floor.

Dr. Jubran: "I told you there is no Grail here. Please leave at once or I will have to call security."

Red Beard, places a large hand on Dr. Jubran's shoulder and looks deep into his eyes. "I will ask you for the second and last time. Where is the Grail?"

Dr. Jubran: "I gave it back. The Armenian antique dealer was here this afternoon and took it."

The bearded man gives Dr. Jubran another piercing look before he takes his hand off of his shoulder, turns around, and leaves. He picks up the crowbar leaning by the door and stuffs it through the handles blocking the door from being opened from the inside. He then goes down the stairs and walks to his car. He opens the trunk and takes out a large plastic jerrycan. He then returns to the building, enters, and heads up the stairs with the container, to the fourth floor.

34

At The Small Café Near the TV Station. Ilana Questions Yigal About His Meeting with the Military Rabbi

Ilana: "What do you make of Rabbi Amar?"

Yigal: "During our conversation, he sounded quite convincing...."

Ilana: "But?"

Yigal: "It seems Mr. Amar wasn't 100% accurate." Yigal places a black-and-white photo on the table.

Ilana: "What are we looking at?"

Yigal: "This photograph was taken by the soldier from Unit 669. The figures are very blurry, however, look here, on the left side. Do you see that man, with the beard?"

Ilana: "Rabbi Amar?"

Yigal: "That's right. In the foreground, you can clearly see the bodies laid out in a row before they were put into the bags."

Ilana: "So?"

Yigal: "So, as you probably remember, in the interview, the Rabbi said that he arrived at the scene after the corpses had already been put into sealed bags – and thus he could not have seen whether the Grail was in the grasp of any of the corpses."

Ilana: "So the Rabbi is lying!"

Yigal: "Unless you have another explanation."

Ilana: "Do you think the Rabbi is the one who took the goblet?"

Yigal: "There is of course no evidence to that. Nevertheless, the fact that the Rabbi wasn't forthcoming about his presence at the site raises some questions."

Ilana: "Doctor Ernan said that the medallion you gave him was the second goblet he had seen. Could it be that the Rabbi brought him the goblet found in the cave to be examined?"

Yigal: "That wouldn't be improbable."

Ilana, turning to face the camera: "And so, like the Knights of the Round Table, we continued our unrelenting search for the Holy Grail. We decided to take a few steps back, to the Technion Institute's isotope lab. We intended to further question Doctor Ernan regarding the "second goblet." However, when we returned to the Technion, a surprise was awaiting."

35

Once Again at the Technion Laboratories

The entrance to the laboratory building at the Technion is closed off by police barricades. The front of the building is covered in soot, and the fourth-floor windows are broken. Two uniformed police officers stand next to the entrance. Ilana approaches them.

Police officer: "Sorry, no entry allowed."

Ilana: "What happened here?"

Police officer: "There was a fire last night."

Ilana: "When did that happen?"

Police officer: "We've been here all night. The firefighters have already left."

Ilana: "Do you know what burned down?"

Police officer: "I really don't."

Ilana: "I'm from the TV..."

Police officer: "Sorry, I was instructed to not let anybody in."

Ilana: "Who gave you that order? I'd like to speak with them."

At that moment, Victor Elbar steps out of the building and walks toward the gate.

Victor, to the police officers at the gate: "It's okay." To

Ilana: "Hello Ilana, it's been a while. Wow! What have you done to your hair?"

Ilana: "I read somewhere that men prefer blondes."

Victor: "I didn't know that you were interested in men," he turns to the camera operator: "Why are you filming me? Film her, you don't even notice what a beauty you have here... such a waste."

Ilana: "Have you found the Holy Grail?"

Victor: "Gale? Who is Gale?"

Ilana: "Come on Victor, we've already agreed that acting is not your forté. Have you found the Grail?"

Victor: "I swear on your mother's life that I have no clue what you're talking about."

Ilana: "I think that you do. And leave my mother out of this."

Victor: "Sorry... get in touch with me later. We can grab a coffee together... maybe something will come to me by then."

Superintendent Victor climbs into his car and drives off. Ilana calls Yigal on her mobile phone.

Ilana: "Yigal, I am at the Technion right now. There was a fire in the lab building. The police are here, they're not letting me in. I want you to go immediately to the firefighters HQ in Haifa and try and figure out what's going on."

36

At the Fire Station

The fire station is buzzing. Firefighters are busy rolling up firehoses and organizing gear spread out on the ground. Yigal arrives with the broadcast vehicle. He enters the building and walks down a corridor, arriving at the station chief's office. The door is open. The station chief is sitting behind his desk. There are several other firefighters in the room.

Yigal: "Good morning."

Station Chief: "Good morning. May I ask who you are?"

Yigal: "We're from Channel One – about the fire at the Technion. We were supposed to shoot there for a TV program."

Station Chief: "Looks like someone had other plans..."

Yigal: "It seems so. What exactly happened there?"

Station Chief: "It's still too early to tell. It could very well be arson."

Yigal: "At the Isotopes Lab?"

Station Chief, to his deputy: "Where was the source of the fire?"

Deputy: "At the Genetics lab."

Yigal: "Are you sure? Not at the Isotopes Lab?"

Deputy: "Yes, I just got back from there. The fire broke out on the fourth floor, at the Genetics lab."

Yigal: "The Isotopes Lab is on the second floor."

Deputy: "If you say so. Anyway, there was no significant damage to the second floor."

Yigal: "Is the police conducting an arson investigation?"

Station Chief: "No. Fire investigations are in our jurisdiction."

Yigal: "So why are the police there?"

Station Chief: "Suspected murder!"

Yigal: "Murder? What murder? Who was murdered?"

Station Chief: "I'm afraid I'm not at liberty to give you any details on that. You'll have to ask the police... Anyway, I don't know much either, not beyond the obvious fact that the Genetics lab burned down."

Yigal: "Are you sure that the fire broke out on the fourth floor and not the second?"

The firefighters gaze impatiently at Yigal.

Yigal: "Okay. Alright. Thank you."

Station Chief: "Have a great day... it really is about time someone made a program about us..."

37

The Cemetery in Haifa. The President of the Technion gives a Eulogy Over an Open Grave

President: "We are here today to pay our respects to one of Israel's most promising scientists. Despite his young age, Dr. Salim Jubran was among the best scientists in the world studying the human genome. His research acquired him a great reputation across the globe, and he was even mentioned as a potential candidate for a Nobel Prize. We are proud that Dr. Jubran began his journey at our institution, and are deeply sad he ended it prematurely, in these tragic events.

Personally, I am proud to have known him, to have been in his presence, and witnessed his exceptional character. I am sure that Dr. Salim Jubran's legacy, that of inquisitiveness, of trailblazing exploration, and creativity, will be a beacon for many more students and researchers.

This morning, I called the Senate Committee to a special meeting. We decided to commemorate Dr. Jubran, may he rest in peace, by naming the Genetics lab after him once we finish the renovation work scheduled to start tomorrow.

On behalf of the Technion's faculty and students, I send my condolences to Salim's wife, his children, his parents, and his entire family. Be proud of his memory, which we will forever cherish in our hearts."

Standing in the crowd Yigal recognizes Dr. Ernan, the Head of the Isotopes Department.

Yigal and his crew return to the cemetery parking lot. Yigal sits in the driver's seat, while the crew gets into the backseats. Just as Yigal reaches out to start the engine, Dr. Ernan squeezes into the vehicle and sits next to him.

Dr. Ernan: "Do you remember me?"

Yigal:" Of course, you're the head of the Isotopes Department."

Dr. Ernan: "Remember when you asked me about the other goblet?"

Yigal: "Yes. You told me, or rather implied, that you were brought another one for examination."

Dr. Ernan: "Indeed. Two weeks ago, the other goblet was brought to me to determine its age."

Yigal: "Who brought it to you? A military rabbi, perhaps?"

Dr. Ernan: "A military rabbi? No! Why? It was brought to me by an Armenian antiquities dealer from downtown Haifa. The Technion provides these lab services also to private entities and individuals. This dealer occasionally brings me antiques for dating and authentication."

Yigal: "And did you check it?"

Dr. Aran: "Yes. The goblet was dated to the Second Temple period. Meaning, about two thousand years ago."

Yigal: "Interesting."

Dr. Ernan: "Yes, but this isn't what I'm here for. Two days ago, I sat in the cafeteria with Dr. Jubran. We're old friends. I told him about the grail, and the inscription engraved on it 'Jesus Nazarenus.' After we finished our coffee, Dr. Jubran asked to see it, and came with me to my lab. It was after I had finished the tests. He asked that I give him the grail for a few hours so he could check 'something.' I asked him what that 'something' was, but he just smiled and did not answer. As you know, Dr. Jubran was a Christian Arab born in Nazareth, so it only seemed natural for him to show interest."

Yigal: "And you still don't know what Dr. Jubran did with it in the genetics lab?"

Dr. Ernan: "Not a clue. Honestly, I was going to ask, but I never got a chance."

Yigal: "Do you know the name of the antique dealer?"

Dr. Ernan: "Of course, Yosef Khachaturian. Khachaturian – like the famous composer."

Yigal: "Where is the antique store?"

Dr. Ernan: "I don't remember the exact address. It's downtown... I can check..."

Yigal: "It's okay... why do you tell me all this?

Dr. Ernan: "I don't know. I know that you're investigating this Grail business. I suddenly remembered that it was also at Jubran's lab. They're saying the fire was intentional – arson... you see, Dr. Jubran was a close friend of mine... I have a bad feeling about this... and I have a feeling that it all has something to do with this cursed object."

Yigal: "Why do you say the object is cursed?"

Dr. Ernan: "Because it seems that all who touch it die an unnatural death."

Yigal: "All who touch it?"

Dr. Ernan: "Yes. If it truly is the Holy Grail, then first Jesus, then the old man from the cave the plane crashed into... Oh, yes, I saw your show from two weeks ago, and now Dr. Jubran."

Yigal: "I went to the fire station. They claim that the fire was not accidental, but arson. Meaning – murder."

Dr. Ernan: "This whole business seems completely crazy to me."

Yigal: "If it truly is arson, it could certainly have something to do with the Grail. The question is what

Dr. Jubran was checking. Can you guess?"

Dr. Ernan: "Absolutely not. Dr. Jubran studied the human genome. However, as I said, he was also Christian, and it is natural he would be interested in such an object."

Yigal: "The problem is, it's too late to ask him now."

Dr. Ernan: "Maybe Dina would know."

Yigal: "Dina?"

Dr. Ernan: "Dina... the assistant, his research assistant."

Yigal: "Dinah who?"

Dr. Ernan: "I do not know. I only know her by her first name. However, it shouldn't be a problem to check with the staff administration."

38

Ilana and Yigal – Another Attempt to Assemble the Pieces.

Ilana: "It seems that instead of connecting the pieces, we are occupied with more and more new pieces which are appearing in this puzzle."

Yigal: "Yes. I feel as if we're fighting some sort of Hydra. That multi-headed mythological monster. In place of every head, we successfully sever, three new ones immediately grow."

Ilana: "And as Dr. Ernan said, it looks like the Holy Grail is starting to – or rather continuing to – take on lives...

The truth is, I have thought of just leaving the matter alone. Hand in all the material we've gathered to the police. Let them continue the investigation, which already has elements that could have criminal ramifications."

Yigal: "Even so, I am confused as to why the goblet was taken to the fourth floor. I have been racking my brain – what does the Holy Grail have to do with a young scientist, a Nobel Prize candidate, studying the human genome?"

Ilana: "The question is what do we know, or rather, what we do not know about the Grail."

Yigal: "Clearly, there is a mysterious missing link between the two researchers, and the two laboratories – just two floors away from each other yet dealing with such different fields that could not be further from each other."

Ilana: "And that takes us back to the beginning, meaning, to Professor Shmaryahu Rothman."

39

Yigal Rings the Doorbell at Professor Shmaryahu Rothman's House. The Professor's wife, Leah, Opens the Door

Yigal: "Good morning."

Leah, suspicious: "Good... Mor...ning."

Yigal: "Thank you for agreeing to meet us again."

Leah:" You promised me it would be the last time. Even when my husband won the Israel Prize, we were not blessed three times by the presence of TV crews. Calling loudly: "Shmaryahu!... Steven Spielberg and his Hollywood team are here again...."

Shmaryahu enters wearing slippers, with his hair unkempt.

Leah, scolding him: "You could have at least combed your hair if you're going on television." To the crew: "Wait, don't start filming." Bringing a brush and comb, she begins brushing her husband's thin white hair, as he squirms, struggling to escape. "Old men are just like babies." Leah complains.

Shmaryahu: "Leah, my dear, do you not see that these nice people are drooling at the thought of your wonderful cookies? Perhaps you could stop keeping them waiting?"

Leah scurries away, mumbling complaints under her breath.

Shmaryahu: Turning toward the crew with a kindly smile. "Well? What has your hunt after the Holy Grail surfaced?"

Yigal: "For now it seems that more than us hunting the Grail, it has been hunting us."

Shmaryahu: "Enlighten me?"

Yigal: "As far as we know, the goblet that was found in the cave at Hosha somehow fell into the hands of an Armenian antique dealer in Haifa. I don't want to slander anyone however, one can only assume that a rescue or military servicemember that was on site, took the grail and sold it to the dealer."

Shmaryahu: "Do you know this dealer's name? Could it be my old friend Khachaturian?"

Yigal, surprised: "You know him?"

Shmaryahu: "I've known him for decades. Quite the shady fellow, but I must say, extremely knowledgeable."

Yigal: "The Armenian took the goblet to be examined at the Technion."

Shmaryahu: "Indeed, this is a common, routine procedure. What did the lab find?"

Yigal: "Dr. Ernan found that the object is from the Second Temple period, meaning the time of Jesus."

Shmaryahu is excited: "Very interesting... super interesting! Even though dozens or even hundreds of goblets like this one were produced and despite the fact that any attribution of the grail to Jesus is no more than wild speculation."

Yigal: "Do you remember the words inscribed on the old man's medallion?"

Shmaryahu: "Jesus Nazarenus? – Of course."

Yigal: "Ernan says these words were also inscribed on this goblet."

Shmaryahu: "Incredible! Although – again – anyone could have carved these words into it. Anyway, if the results are accurate, and knowing Dr. Ernan, there is no reason to doubt his findings, then we are talking about an ancient object that by law belongs to the state. Mr. Khachaturian probably purchased it from a soldier for pennies."

Leah returns bearing a tray topped with a bowl of cookies, a pitcher of lemonade, and cups.

Leah: "Help yourself. Shmaryahu, I'm reminding you that we need to leave in forty minutes."

Yigal, takes a cookie: "Thank you. Truly wonderful cookies. We will be done shortly."

Leah: "I'm going to get ready. The Professor also needs to get dressed."

Shmaryahu: Setting the half-eaten cookie aside, he mumbles to himself: "Dreadful cookies," continuing: "So where is the goblet now?"

Yigal: "After the tests at the Isotopes Lab, Dr. Ernan gave it to his friend, Dr. Salim Jubran, the head of the Genetics lab. The lab is two floors above Dr. Ernan's lab.

Shmaryahu: "Why was it taken to the genetics lab?"

Yigal: "Oh... that is precisely what we came to find out, from you."

Shmaryahu: Muttering to himself: "To the Genetics lab? ... I don't understand."

Yigal: "The head of the lab, Dr. Salim Jubran, was a world-renowned expert of the human genome."

Shmaryahu: "The human genome?... What do you mean was?"

Yigal: "There was a fire at the lab last night. It might have been arson. Dr. Jubran was in the lab at the time. The firefighters found his burnt body."

Shmaryahu: "And the goblet?"

Yigal shrugs.

Shmaryahu sinks into deep thought. Slowly, he straightens his back.

Shmaryahu, in a low voice, speaking slowly and carefully choosing every word: "Yes. There could be an explanation. I can only think of one, but if it is correct, then it is utterly crazy and terrifying... Yes, insane and even extremely dangerous!!!"

40

At the TV Offices. Another Team Meeting.

Attended by Ilan Yafe, the director of programming, and Yehuda Yuval, the CEO of the channel

Ilan: "Well... Yesterday we broke the all-time ratings record for the program."

Ilana: "Taking into account that the broadcast was at the same time as the Tel Aviv soccer tournament, that really is pretty good."

Ilan: "I must say that personally, I found it fascinating... well done."

Ilana: "For some reason, I have the feeling that after such an exciting premier, there should be some sort of anti-climax?"

Ilan: "I wouldn't say that though, you are correct – we have a problem."

Ilana: ????????

Ilan: "You see Ilana, you know you have my full backing..."

Ilana: "But..."

Ilan: "Yes but... Such a small word that causes so many problems. The investigation about your 'Holy Grail' is causing two not-so-small concerns. One is a professional issue, which is easier to discuss, and the other... is political."

Ilana: "Let's start with the professional issue?"

Ilan: "Okay. The problem is that you definitely have succeeded in presenting an outstanding story. In creating suspense and interest, which has been exacerbated by the media. The issue... the question is whether behind all the pyrotechnics, do we actually have any 'meat' to support it?"

"We're creating astronomical expectations... the question is whether the check will clear. To put it simply – if it turns out that we're inflating a colossal bluff, if it turns out that there's no substance to this story, this whole fiasco could blow up in our faces. We'll be slaughtered. Not to mention the credibility of the program itself... And your own personal integrity."

Ilana: "I completely understand what you're saying. The truth is, it's even worse than you think. I want to show you a short segment that has not been broadcast yet. A meeting between our investigator – Yigal – and Professor Shmaryahu Rothman, you remember... the expert on archaeology and Western religions."

41

Back to the meeting between Yigal and Professor Shmaryahu

Yigal: "You said that you might have an explanation as to the link between the Grail and the genetics lab?"

Shmaryahu: "I am not certain one could call it an explanation. It is more like a crazy theory. completely crazy, but it is the only one I can think of. The truth is that I am apprehensive about saying it out loud."

Yigal: "And yet, it may be the only explanation we have."

Shmaryahu: "Well, according to Christian tradition, the same disciple who took the goblet took it with him to Golgotha, where Jesus was crucified. A Roman soldier stabbed Jesus with his spear, known to this day as the 'Holy Lance.' The disciple collected the blood gushing from his teacher's side into the goblet."

Shmaryahu peers at Yigal and Yigal responds with questioning eyes.

Shmaryahu: "Well, my friend... you still don't get it? The bottom of the Holy Grail was stained with the coagulated blood of Christ."

Yigal: "A two-thousand-year-old blood stain?"

Shmaryahu: "Yes. Why not? If my theory about the

people of the Order is right, they would have probably preserved it quite well. It is likely that the old man who you say clung to the Grail, had pulled it out of its hiding place to save it from the collapsing cave."

Yigal: "Ok. So, let's say there is such a stain. What would it mean?"

Shmaryahu, smiling generously: "Oh, come on... you still don't get it, do you? Blood means cells. Cells mean chromosomes. Chromosomes mean genes."

Yigal, frowns and says with evident doubt in his voice: "So you think that Dr. Jubran took the Grail to the genetics lab to run the congealed blood for genetics? What is this... Jurassic Park?"

Shmaryahu: "Not quite Jurassic Park, but if indeed the goblet was sent for genetic testing, that would be the only explanation, to check Jesus' genome."

Yigal: "That sounds totally insane!"

Shmaryahu: "Right. And even more insane than you could possibly imagine."

Yigal: ???

Shmaryahu: "Can we even begin to fathom what this is? Do you remember how Jesus was said to be born? Who his mother was?"

Yigal: "The Virgin Mary."

Shmaryahu: "Right. And how was the virgin made pregnant?"

Yigal: "Ok, I think I'm starting to get it. Someone wants to prove that Jesus had the genome of a normal human. That Mary was not really a virgin and that she was impregnated by a man, the natural way?"

Shmaryahu: "Or... the opposite, that she indeed was impregnated unnaturally.

Yigal: "No, no! That would be really, totally crazy."

Shmaryahu, filled with excitement: "Yes, yes! Oh yes indeed. I see the light bulb is finally turning on. If it wasn't the impotent carpenter nor the neighbor, but rather God, then what they were after at the genetics lab was not only the human genome but the genome of God. **the Genome of God and none other!**"

Yigal: "Oh my God."

Shmaryahu: "Yes, that's the one I am talking about. The genome of God... Jesus' 'biological father'... so to speak"

42
The Discussion Continues in The Production Office

Ilan: "Oh my God! As if we needed even more trouble."

Ilana: "Right. If deciphering God or Jesus' genome is what they were dabbling with at that lab, arson and murder are frivolous matters."

At that moment, Yehuda Yuval, the CEO of the station who was quiet up until now, slaps his hand flat down on the table.

Yehuda: "That's it. This story has really gotten out of hand. A juicy provocative investigation is one thing but declaring an apocalyptic war on half of the world's population is another. What you're cooking up here is no less than waging war against the entire Christian world which as it happens, consists of over two billion believers. From the get-go, this whole Holy Grail thing seemed silly to me. Up until now, this silliness was harmless and even brought in pretty good ratings. Now we've taken it one step too far. We've crossed the line."

Ilana: "But if there is a problem here it is not us who are causing it. We are merely investigating."

Yehuda: "Your program is called 'As a Matter of Fact.'

Fact means facts. Not speculations. So far, you've been creating this elaborate theory about a fabled Grail that you can't even prove exists."

Ilana: "And if we were to find it and present it... here, right here on this table?"

Yehuda: "If... such a small word that makes the huge difference between fantasy and reality."

Ilan: "Wait, Yehuda... why don't we just let them work? Let's say they do manage to prove it... present the facts."

Yehuda: "What do you mean, let them work? Nobody has been fired yet... but from now on, no episode of this show will air without my personal approval. And that includes promos as well. Nothing. Nada. Zilch. Is that clear?"

After these words accompanied by another hard slap on the table, Yehuda gets up and leaves the room.

Ilan: "There you have it, Ilana. You launched your spaceship to astronomical heights and the question now is if you can land it back safely on Earth, or will we all crash and burn with it."

43

A Week After the CEO's Harsh Words, Ilana Goes on Air Once Again

Ilana: "Over three weeks have passed since our last broadcast. The last episode in the Holy Grail saga was delayed and almost canceled. Since the newspapers and the news channels have already discussed it, I will not list all the reasons and circumstances that prevented us from broadcasting.

As you know, it has been claimed that the program could compromise a sensitive police investigation and even vital State interests. We wouldn't be on the air today, if it weren't for public pressure exerted by you, our devoted viewers.

Due to the special circumstances that have unfolded, some of the segments that we will bring here today are reenacted by professional actors."

"We found out that two days before the broadcast of the last episode of the program, a small car made its way up a remote winding road on Mt. Carmel. At the wheel sat Yosef Khachaturian, an antique dealer from downtown Haifa. In the back seat sat a man whom we will call "Red Beard" for now. Red Beard is the pyromaniac caught by the security cameras in the parking lot of the Technion laboratories as well as inside the genetics laboratory.

In this reenactment, "Red Beard" is seen wearing dark glasses, and holding a gun aimed at the head of the actor playing the antique dealer.

Khachaturian: "Where are you taking me?"

Red Beard: "No questions!"

Khachaturian: "You wanted the goblet – it is here," he points to a duffle bag resting on the seat next to him. "What else do you want from me?"

Red Beard: "Pull over here."

Khachaturian: "It is dangerous here... can we go a little further?"

Red Beard, puts the gun to the antique dealer's head: "I said pull over!"

The car stops.

Red Beard, commands: "Get in the back seat."

Khachaturian gets out and then into the back seat. Holding the bag in one hand, the red-bearded man gets out of the vehicle, and before Khachaturian realizes what is happening, he reaches with his other hand through the open window in front and presses the door lock, releases the handbrake, and sends the car off into the ravine.

The red-bearded man walks a few yards down the road, gets into another car parked on the side of the road, and sets off on his way.

44
Yigal Visits the Antiquities Shop

Ilana: "According to Doctor Ernan's testimony, the goblet was supposed to be in the hands of an Armenian antique dealer named Yosef Khachaturian. A few hours before the dramatic events took place as depicted in the reenactment you have just watched, our very own Yigal paid a surprise visit to the antique shop."

The TV van parks right in front of the store. Yigal gets out and heads towards the door. Above the door hangs an old and rusty sign: "Khachaturian – Antiques Trading House. "The shop window is dusty and neglected. Yigal knocks on the closed door several times and then pushes down the handle. The door opens and Yigal enters.

Yigal: "Hello... is there anyone here? Hello?"

Yigal walks around the store. There is nobody there. The shop looks like it had survived an earthquake. Drawers pulled out; cabinet doors wide open, entire shelves thrown to the floor. Various objects are scattered everywhere, pottery fragments... It is clear that someone ripped the place apart in search of something.

Yigal goes behind the counter. On a small table stands an old computer monitor covered in dust. The screen is on. Yigal taps the keyboard. The screen lights up. The screen shows an outgoing e-mail. Yigal opens the attachment. A picture of a goblet appears. Yigal goes back to the previous screen. He looks around and notices a printer. He prints out the e-mail and the photo of the goblet. He folds the pages and puts them in his pocket. He turns off the computer and leaves the store. He crosses the street, approaches the TV van, and pulls his cell phone out of his pocket.

Yigal: "Hey Ilana... I have something!!! I have a picture of the Grail... no, there was nobody there... the store is empty... someone was here before me and did a thorough search. They may have found and taken the Grail. But listen, I need you to urgently look into an e-mail address... Yes, write it down... No, I have no idea who it might be, but it's important... I'll explain later... I'll see you back at the office in two hours."

A minute later Yigal's phone rings

Ilana: "Yigal?"

Yigal: "I'm listening."

Ilana: "The email address you gave me belongs to the Patriarch of the Armenian Church in Jerusalem. Does that fit what you're looking for"

Yigal: "Like a glove."

Ilana: "What is your theory?"

Yigal: "There is no theory here. The antiquities dealer sent the Patriarch a photo of the goblet.

In the e-mail, he writes that he has a certificate from the Technion regarding its age. He doesn't write it explicitly, but it's clear he's offering to sell it. "

Ilana: "Can you interview the dealer?"

Yigal: "That was my intention, but as I said, there is no one here. The place looks like

A bomb blew up in it. I've been waiting for half an hour in the van in front of the store."

Ilana: "It is very important that you manage to interview the dealer. Everything points to him having or having had the goblet.

Yigal: "Hey Ilana... hold on a second... something is happening here. I'm signing off. I'll get back to you soon."

A police car arrives, stops, and parks at the curb, right in front of the door of the shop. Two police officers step out of the car and enter the store. A third police officer remains standing by the vehicle. Yigal approaches the car and turns to the police officer.

Yigal: "Did something happen?"

Police officer: "Who are you?"

Yigal: "Channel One."

Police officer: "What are you doing here?"

Yigal: "Just some research about antiquities. We set up a meeting with the owner of the store, Yosef Khachaturian."

Police officer: "What time did you arrange to meet?"

Yigal: "I've been waiting for him for half an hour."

Police officer: "You can go, he won't be coming."

Yigal: "Why not?"

Police officer: "He was in a car accident."

Yigal: "Is he injured?"

Police officer: "I'm afraid it's worse than that but I'm not at liberty to say. One thing is for sure – he won't be coming here any time today."

45

Ilana Visits the Armenian Church in Jerusalem

Strolling under the high arches with the organ playing and chanting in the background, Ilana dictates into her recorder.

Ilana: "Just as the ripples of the sea erase footprints in the sand, our investigation keeps getting hit by disastrous waves that each time leave us facing a dead end, or rather a dead body.

A plane crash, a fire in a laboratory, a car accident... Are these all coincidences? Is it possible that an invisible hand plays behind this cycle of calamities, or perhaps it is the mystical artifact that was woken up from its two-thousand-year sleep, that is now taking revenge on the disturbers of its rest.

Now, the million-dollar question is: Did the antiquities dealer hand the goblet to the patriarch of the Armenian church?"

The Patriarch finishes Sunday mass and retires to his office. Ilana follows him. One of the priests stops her in front of the office door.

Priest: "Who are you looking for?"

Ilana: "I'm from the TV. I want to talk to the patriarch."

Priest: "Do you have an appointment?"

Ilana: "No, but it will only take a few minutes."

Priest: "Please wait here." The priest enters the room and comes out again a minute later. " His Holiness will see you now."

The patriarch welcomes Ilana warmly.

Ilana: "Your Excellency, thank you for agreeing to see me. May I present you with a number of questions?

The Patriarch, smiles brightly: "Hello there. How may I help you?"

Ilana: "We are conducting an investigation on the Holy Grail as I am sure you must have heard by now."

The Patriarch: "Yes, though I do not watch TV, but I would love to hear what you know. Is there any truth to the rumor that the Grail has been found?"

Ilana: "Are you familiar with the name Yosef Khachaturian?"

The Patriarch: "Khachaturian... I have never met the man. I understand that he is an antique dealer. We have received several inquiries from him. He claims to have in his possession, an ancient goblet and has offered to sell it to the church. In the only telephone conversation I had with him, I asked him to agree to meet with the Church's experts. I even contacted the Vatican for this purpose. We must be very careful when it comes to matters such as this."

Ilana: "And then what happened?"

The Patriarch: "After that phone call I didn't hear from him again. I assume it must have been some sort of a scam. I hold no one to blame. I believe the dealer was misled by someone else and surely acted in good faith. Anyway, he didn't get back to me."

Ilana: "Do you believe that the Holy Grail exists?"

The Patriarch: "Certainly. I believe that the goblet from which the savior drank did indeed exist. Should the Grail be discovered someday, I would love to see and hold it. Nevertheless, I'm afraid that the matter you are dealing with is nothing more than a deal gone sour at the very best, or a sophisticated fraud attempt at the very worst."

Ilana: "Do you know that the antique dealer is no longer alive?"

The Patriarch, surprised: "What do you mean, 'not alive?'"

Ilana: "He was killed in a car accident. Two days ago. His car skidded into a ravine on Mt. Carmel. Maybe that is why he was incommunicado."

The Patriarch: "Sad news, I shall pray for him."

Ilana: "So, before he died, he offered to sell the goblet to you?"

The Patriarch: "Not to me. I told him right away that I don't consider myself qualified to deal with such things. I offered to relay the message to the Vatican, on the condition that he would agree to have the goblet inspected by experts on behalf of the church. "

Ilana: "Did he name his price?"

The Patriarch: "Oh... no... we didn't get to talk about money at all... and you? Have you seen the goblet?"

Ilana: "No. I didn't see it, I thought I might find it here."

The Patriarch, with his kind smile: "I would have gladly shown it to you, alas, I cannot help you with that."

Ilana and the patriarch look at each other in silence in what seems to be a face-off.

Ilana: "Thank you for agreeing to speak with me."

The Patriarch: "If you find the goblet, I will be grateful for the privilege of seeing it in person."

Ilana: "I promise. Thank you very much for your time."

46
At the President's Residence, Jerusalem. Dozens of Journalists and TV Crews are Preparing for A Press Conference. Ilana and her Team are there too.

Ilana: "It looks like the Vatican doesn't waste any time. Only two days after our meeting with the Armenian Patriarch, we were informed about a possible visit of the Vatican's Cardinal Secretary of State as the President's personal guest."

The Executive Director of the President's Residence steps up to the microphone.

Executive Director: "The President will deliver a short speech. After that, he will address a number of your questions. Please, Mr. President."

The director steps off the podium. The President enters and approaches the heap of microphones.

The President: "Good evening. A few months ago, I met with the Pope at the Vatican. During our conversation, the Pope expressed his warm feelings toward the Jewish people and the State of Israel, as well as his wish to promote peace and understanding between religions and believers. At the end of the meeting, I invited the Pope to visit Israel, the Holy Land."

"A number of days ago, I received an official letter from the Holy See, in which the Pope expressed his regret for not being able to respond to my invitation in the near future, yet he wishes to send his personal secretary and the Vatican Secretary of State, the Honorable Cardinal Mr. Roberto Aluffi to Israel for a special visit.

In coordination with the Prime Minister and the Minister of Foreign Affairs, yesterday, I issued an official invitation for a visit that will take place in the coming days. A preparatory team on behalf of the Vatican will arrive in Israel tomorrow. I view this visit as extremely significant, a message of understanding and tolerance continuing the two-thousand-year-old dialogue between the Jewish people and the Christian world."

The President ends his brief message, and it is now time for questions.

Reporter: "Mr. President, will you mention before the Cardinal the issue of our missing soldiers?"

The President: "I have discussed this issue with the Pope during my visit to the Vatican. The Pope expressed his sympathies with the families and promised his influence, to do as much as he can. The Prime Minister and I both intend to raise this issue once again."

Ilana: "Is there any connection between the Cardinal's visit at this time and the story of the 'Holy Grail' that has recently made headlines?"

The President: "As I mentioned at the beginning of my remarks, I extended this invitation several months ago. With all due respect, it seems to me that despite all the exoticism that has recently been buzzing around as regards rumors about the Holy Grail, the whole thing is nothing but a tempest in a teapot or rather in a goblet. The honorable Cardinal is coming to our country to visit holy Christian sites bearing messages of peace and friendship."

Ilana walks away and quietly faces the camera

Ilana: "Well then, the President dismisses any ties between the Cardinal's visit and the matter of the Holy Grail, while reliable sources confirm such a connection does in fact exist. Our sources have revealed that the Holy See sent a secret message to the Israeli government, in which he stated that the Grail is one of the main issues the Cardinal shall discuss during his visit to Israel. Despite all attempts to cover this up, it seems that the Vatican has hard evidence concerning the Grail. This includes photographs which were apparently sent to the Vatican by the Armenian Patriarch, who received them from an antiquities dealer whose death is still under police investigation."

47

In the Mysterious Basement in Jerusalem. The Committee Reconvenes

The Chairman, MK Zeev: "Well gentlemen, I can now say that indeed the artifact they call the 'Holy Grail' has been found. Furthermore, thanks to some actions, it is now in our possession."

One of the Rabbis: "What do you mean 'in our possession'?"

The Chairman places the duffle bag taken from the Armenian dealer on the table. He pulls out the goblet and places it on the table.

Rabbi Pinchas, known for his extreme opinions gets up and bangs on the table.

Rabbi Pinchas: "We must destroy this thing immediately."

MK Zeev: "According to experts, this is an artifact from the days of the Second Temple. This is truly a significant and most rare archeological find."

Rabbi Pinchas: "This thing is a recipe for destruction. Nothing good will come out of it. I say we should destroy it right here, right now.

MK Zeev: "Calm down, Rabbi Pinchas..."

Rabbi Pinchas: "And why should I do that? This is not the time for liberalism... have you lost sight? We must destroy this thing. The sooner the better! Before it destroys us!"

MK Zeev: "Please sit sir. Wise words are heard when they are said peacefully. Let us hear what others have to say."

Committee member: "I truly understand our friend Rabbi Pinchas' concern. He is worried that revealing this object will lead to a wave of revival throughout the Christian world which will resurface old fears and hatred. Nevertheless, I say that this artifact might be a good thing. It is quite possible that it could serve as a bridge between faiths and peoples."

Rabbi Arieh: "Let's not be naïve. Things cannot be undone. From the moment this object sees the light of day, it will never be tucked away again. There are already rumors going about."

MK Zeev: "Rumors, fables about the Grail have been circling the globe for two thousand years. If they continue for two thousand more, what difference would it make?"

Rabbi Arieh: "Gentlemen, you are contradicting yourselves. If it cannot be made to go away, how do you expect to hide it being destroyed? Sooner or later, it will be made known to all. Jews will be blamed once again. It will cause a great commotion, even bloodshed".

MK Zeev: "There, there now... slow down..."

Rabbi Arieh: "Gentlemen, I speak not out of anger but from true fear. We must keep ourselves from rash actions that can never be reversed. I think that at the very least, we should ask the Grand – 'Gadol' – Rabbi for his decisive word."

Silence envelopes the room. The Chairman strokes his beard as he ponders.

MK Zeev: "I agree with Arieh. Let us bring this matter before the Gadol."

The chairman looks around him and sees agreeing nods. The men get up and shake hands. They bid their farewells and sneak out of the basement into the darkness.

48
At the Office of Mr. Yoram Shalev, Director General of the Israel Ministry of Foreign Affairs

Present at the meeting: The Director General, Mr. Ofer Levi – Deputy Director General, Mr. Alessandro Contorno – the Vatican ambassador to Israel, and the Armenian Patriarch.

The Director General: "On behalf of the President of the State of Israel, the Prime Minister, and the people of Israel, I would like to thank His Holiness for his decision to bless us with the presence of his special emissary here in the Holy land. I am sure that this visit shall further strengthen the remarkable relations between Israel and the Vatican."

Vatican ambassador: "Director General, Mr. Shalev. Thank you for your warm welcome. His Holiness has asked me to convey his gratitude to the President and the Prime Minister for their generous invitation and sends his warm blessings to the People of Israel."

Director General: "I have appointed Mr. Levi to head the Ministry of Foreign Affairs planning team. He will be in constant contact with you, for all the preparations that will be required for this important visit."

Vatican ambassador: "Our team headed by Mr. Olivetti will arrive tomorrow. Mr. Olivetti has been granted full authority to coordinate all aspects of this visit. As for today, I have requested His Excellency the head of the Armenian Patriarchate of Jerusalem, to join me for good reason... with your permission."

Director General: "Please."

Vatican ambassador: "Recently, one of your TV programs reported about the finding of a highly significant archaeological artifact, more specifically, the Holy Grail. His Holiness expressed much interest in this matter."

Director General: "Yes, I also heard about this, though I must tell you that apart from a high ratings TV story, we do not have any evidence that such an object was indeed unearthed."

Vatican ambassador: "I believe that my colleague here has something to show you..."

The Patriarch pulls out of his bag the photo of the goblet that was emailed to him by the antique dealer and places it on the table:

"I received this picture a few days ago from an antiquities dealer in the city of Haifa. The dealer claims that he submitted the goblet to the Technion Institute for examination where it was dated approximately two thousand years old. The dealer offered to sell the artifact."

Director General: "Did you purchase it?"

The Patriarch: "We considered to do it, legally of course, but then something happened."

Director General: ?????????

The Patriarch: The dealer was found dead following a road accident and the goblet disappeared.

Director General: "This is very strange. I must admit that all this information is absolutely new to me. I will undertake to inquire after this matter, and I'll let you know what I was able to find."

The two church servants thank the Director General. He walks them out and they part ways with a handshake.

49

Ilana, Yigal, and an Unknown Young Woman Sit on The Studio Panel

Ilana: "Well, we seem to be running around in circles, up and down a labyrinth of dead ends. The old man from the hospital disappeared and despite all of our efforts, we could not trace his whereabouts. The Armenian antiquities dealer who had the goblet and even took photos of it was killed in a freak car accident if indeed it was an accident. The human genome research laboratory at the Technion, where the goblet was last seen by Dr. Ernan, caught fire and Dr. Jubran perished in the blaze. Apparently, we have reached many milestones, but the road itself remains shrouded in fog."

Yigal: "Yes, so we had apparently reached an impasse, but just as we thought that the plot that started with a loud fanfare had begun to fade, we caught a really big fish."

Ilana: "You, the viewers at home must be asking, who is the fine young lady sitting here."

Yigal: "Please introduce yourself."

Dina: "Dina... I prefer not to disclose my last name."

Ilana: "You were the late Dr. Jubran's lab assistant."

Dina: "Correct."

Ilana: "I know that you really didn't want to be here at the studio tonight. Why did you decide to come anyway?"

Dina: "That's right. I was reluctant to come here tonight and in fact, I am still not completely okay with it. Still, there are two decisive factors here: first, I think I owe it to Dr. Jubran who was a good man whose loss is still hard for me to come to terms with. Second, there are findings here that were not fully deciphered, and we researchers have no right to hide them from the rest of the world, certainly not from the scientific community."

Ilana: "You mean findings related to the Holy Grail."

Dina: "Findings related to the goblet given to Dr. Jubran for examination."

Ilana: "Did you and Dr. Jubran test genetic material sampled from the goblet?"

Dina: "We did."

Ilana: "Can you elaborate on that?"

Dina: "Certainly. The object you call the Holy Grail was brought to the lab..."

Ilana: "By whom?"

Dina: "I don't know. It was given to Dr. Jubran."

Ilana shows Dina the photo from the Armenian dealer's computer.

Ilana: "Is that the Grail in question?"

Dina: "I cannot say for sure, but it certainly does look like it."

Ilana: "Well, what was the substance you tested?"

Dina: "On the underside of the goblet, practically its entire bottom third was covered in a black stain. We were told it could be congealed blood."

Ilana: "Jesus' blood?"

Dina: "I can only talk about scientific facts. I don't know whose blood it was, but the test concluded it was human blood cells – red and white cells."

Ilana: "And were you able to scrape off blood from the goblet for examination?"

Dina: "Yes, there are several ways to extract and sample organic materials."

Ilana: "So you checked the cells' genetic structure. Do you have the results?"

Dina: "No, I don't have the test results. When I left the lab, we did not yet have a full decryption. I went home around six in the evening. Dr. Jubran was very excited and eager to continue going through the findings and insisted on staying."

Ilana: "And what happened with the findings? Were they destroyed in the fire?"

Dina: "There is no doubt that the data printouts and in fact the computer itself all caught fire, but the Technion's server might have the data backed up.

Ilana: "And can it be found there?"

Dina: "Not anymore. I tried. It's not there."

Ilana: "What does that mean?"

Dina: "I guess someone removed it. After the fire, I was questioned by... Actually, I don't know by whom, there were two of them, maybe the police... or Secret Service.

I told them everything. They put special emphasis on these findings in their investigation. I told them there was a backup. I believe they deleted it or transferred it... Anyway – I checked, it no longer exists."

Ilana: "And what can you remember from the material?"

Dina: "Oh... I have to be very careful here. The findings were definitely unexpected, unusual I mean."

Ilana: "In what sense?"

Dina: "In the sense that according to the genetic structure, there is no doubt that these are cells taken from a human body..."

Ilana: "A human being like you and I."

Dina: "Yes... and no. That's exactly the problem. It was human, no doubt. And yet, the genetic structure was different from yours or mine."

Ilana: "I know that this is a very complicated scientific issue that neither our viewers nor myself are qualified to discuss. Nevertheless, I ask that you try to explain to us in a simple way even if it is not accurate, what was so special about the genome of that human being, whose blood cells you tested."

Dina: "It's really a complex issue, we didn't have time to run all the tests, and as I told you, I left and went home in the middle of the process. It should also be taken into account that this biological material is very old, and some of it might be contaminated."

Ilana: "And with all that, you found something strange...
Please continue."

Dina: "To simply put it, as we all know, each cell of our
body, including white blood cells, has 46 chromosomes.
Two of them determine the sex of the person. That is,
two type X chromosomes mean female, and when one
of the chromosomes is type Y, it is male."

Ilana: "And what did you find in the sample? XX or "XY

Dina: "Well, not quite."

Ilana: "Ok?"

Dina: "We found one type X chromosome, with
completely standard genetic segments. The second
chromosome, however, had a different genetic structure
than what is known to us."

Ilana: "Please try to elaborate – in a simple way of
course."

Dina: "The second chromosome included a number of
segments with characteristics similar to Y, but it differed
from a normal chromosome in two characteristics. The
first is the length of the chromosome, that is, the number
of genetic combinations. Normal Y chromosomes have
a typical length, and they include in their segments
genetic features that have evolved and accumulated over
millions of years. This chromosome was much longer

than a normal chromosome, in fact, it was built in a cyclic fashion that gave it a seemingly infinite length... so to speak. The second phenomenon we identified was that the genes, or genetic segments, had versatile properties that exceeded those of normal genes. That is to say, each gene, or genetic segment, is responsible for determining a certain trait, but the genes in the chromosome that Dr. Jubran called Chromosome Z, were arranged in such a way that the number of traits that each gene section can control was exceptionally large. Infinite, compared to a normal gene."

Ilana: "According to what you are saying, perhaps it is more appropriate to call this miraculous chromosome, 'Chromosome G' – 'the GOD chromosome'?"

Dina, smiles bashfully: "Yes, in terms of the versatility, creativity, and potential infinity of the chromosome... you might be right."

Ilana: "What conclusions or hypotheses did you and Dr. Jubran come up with based on these surprising findings..."

Dina opens her mouth to answer, but Ilana interrupts her with a sharp wave of her hand, and puts her palm over her concealed earpiece. She listens for a few seconds, and then says:

Ilana: "Dear viewers, I am being informed that we are forced to interrupt our program... I apologize, I'm being told that a court injunction order has arrived forbidding us to resume our broadcast."

Ilana continues to listen, and she is obviously mortified.

Ilana: "Well, that's it then. As I said – we cannot continue the broadcast right now. I don't know at this moment what it is all about. I apologize to all of you, dear viewers, and hope we get an explanation soon. "

50

The Next Day. Press Conference. Behind the Microphones Sit the Director of Programming, Ilan, and Ilana

Ilan: "Last night we witnessed an unusual incident when our program "As a Matter of Fact" was interrupted due to an injunction issued by the Jerusalem District Court. As far as I can recall, this is an unprecedented event. We are holding this press conference because of the pressure you members of the press have exerted on us on behalf of the public. I would like to make it clear that we here at Channel One have nothing to hide. However, since this matter is currently being discussed in court, we might not be able to answer all of your questions. Yes..."

Reporter: "Do you know, and can you tell us who is behind the injunction?"

Ilan: "Yes. The injunction was requested by the Attorney General on behalf of the government of the State of Israel."

Reporter: "In the excerpt that was published, it was claimed among other things that the program dealt with a delicate matter that could harm the country's foreign relations. Can you explain what that means?"

Ilan: "That question should be directed to the plaintiff."

Reporter: "The interrupted interview discussed decoding the genome of blood cells found on a goblet that you referred to in recent programs as the "Holy Grail." Is the intention of the program to prove or disprove the Christian claim or belief that Mary, the mother of Jesus to whom the blood stain is attributed, conceived in an unnatural way?"

Ilana: "I am not an expert on theology or Christianity. We had no intention to discuss matters of religion or to hurt the feelings of any religious group. You might recall that we started the investigation with a mystery concerning five graves of unknown persons killed in an Air Force plane crash."

Reporter: "Is the injunction related to the upcoming visit of the Pope's emissary?"

Ilan: "That too is a question that should be directed to the plaintiff."

Reporter: "Do you intend to try to remove the injunction?"

Ilan: "It is a temporary injunction filed with only one party present. It will be brought to the court with both parties involved next Tuesday. I am sure that by then, the Channel's board will have consulted with its legal advisors and formulated its position."

51

The Plane of the Holy See lands at Ben Gurion Airport

All of the dignitaries stand in a line along the Red Carpet. The Cardinal steps off the plane and passes before the greeting dignitaries. When he reaches the Armenian Patriarch, he leans forward to him, and the two whisper for a few seconds. The Cardinal continues to shake hands with the rest. The handshaking ceremony is finished. A convoy of black cars sets off on its journey.

52

At the home of the Grand 'Gadol' Rabbi Shlomo Elnathan, Bnei-Brak

Committee Chairman, MK Zeev: "Your honor, we have come for your advice on a matter of the utmost importance."

Rabbi Shlomo: "What a blessing it is that there are still matters of importance left in the world, otherwise I would not have the opportunity to see your delightful faces."

MK Zeev: "His honor must have heard about the object some call the Holy Grail. Well, I shall not bother you with the details, but circumstances have brought the object to our possession and scientific examinations have confirmed that it is indeed an artifact dated back to the days of the Second Temple, may we live to see it rebuilt."

Rabbi Shlomo and Rabbi Arieh: "Amen"

MK Zeev: "And now, our committee is at odds regarding what we must do with the object. Some are of the opinion that it should be destroyed immediately or it will provoke and evoke differences between the Jewish people and the nations of the world, while others, such as our distinguished colleague here Rabbi Arieh, think the contrary."

Rabbi Shlomo looks up with heavy eyes at Rabbi Arieh.

Rabbi Arieh: "If I may. I believe that destroying the object will be disastrous as it could never be kept a secret. Rumors will travel. News of the find has already gained traction in their newspapers and the television programs they watch. Let us not pour newly found guilt on our heads for the Christian world to blame us for a deed that can never be undone."

MK Zeev: "It is natural for humans to magnify everything that is hidden from view, rather than covet what is already in their custody. All of this object's power is in the fact that it is hidden, but once it will be made visible, it will once again be nothing but a mere instrument. Moreover, I fear that maybe some hostile entity is testing us, and trying to create a provocation designed to slander us before the whole world."

The Grand Rabbi: "Meaning, we should return it to them?"

The Chairman and Rabbi Arieh stare quietly at the Grand Rabbi. Silence grows and then Rabbi Arieh adds –

Rabbi Arieh: "If I may. It would be best to hand the artifact to an authority of their choosing. Otherwise, we might get entangled in their internal conflicts, and we would not want for the cause of the wrath of either party to be attributed to the Jews."

The Grand Rabbi: "Meaning?"

Rabbi Arieh: "It has been reported that in a few days, an emissary from Rome will be arriving in our country. It seems fitting to me that the President should hand it to him in an official, well-documented ceremony. That way we do away with it and even earn their gratitude and support."

The Grand Rabbi, strokes his beard for a while before he says: "I have given great consideration to the wise words of both of you, so I decide and order you to burn and destroy this impure thing. Such artifacts bring no blessings." The old man raises his voice, "Do not hesitate anymore! You must make haste and burn it tonight before it sees tomorrow's light."

53

In the Car Making its Way from Bnei-Brak to Jerusalem, the Two Committee Members Discuss their Meeting with the Grand Rabbi

Rabbi Arieh: "Well, what do you think we should do?"

MK Zeev: "Do we have a choice? You heard the Rabbi."

Rabbi Arieh: "By what you said to the Rabbi, it is clear you feel differently."

MK Zeev: "My opinion does not matter. Here, driving this car – would it matter if I felt differently than the law? Can I drive as I wish regardless of their rules?"

Rabbi Arieh: "I beg your pardon, Sir. It is well known how loyal I am and always have been to you. Even when we were at odds, I always respected and did things your way. But this time... what we are dealing with this time, bears grave global implications. I beseech you... please... wait a little longer. There is still room to consult with more minds. The deed can be done the next day, but once it is done – we will never be able to undo it."

MK Zeev: "My dear friend Rabbi Arieh, your words seem to come from a cautious, loyal heart, no doubt. I give you my word that I shall consider them carefully. Here, we've arrived at your home. Your wife must be worried about you. There she is, waiting by the door.

Rabbi Arieh gets out of the car and climbs the stairs to his apartment. The car drives off.

#   #   #

Rabbi Arieh enters his apartment. He exchanges a few trivial words with his wife. He searches for the cordless telephone, takes it to the bedroom, dials and waits...

Rabbi Arieh: "Yehuda? Good evening... I must speak with you on an urgent matter... no... not in my house... no... yes... I will be there in half an hour."

He comes out of the bedroom and into the living room. He puts on his coat and hat.

Wife: "Leaving already? You've just come home. I have dinner on the stove."

Rabbi Arieh: "Such a woman of valor. I will only be gone an hour. Please wait for me and we will dine together."

54

A Black Car is Passing Slowly Down Mea-Shearim Street

The driver is Yehuda, head of the Jewish department in the General Home Security Service. By his side in the passenger's seat is superintendent Victor Elbar. Together, they listen to the midnight news on the radio. The narrator is talking about the visit of the Pope's emissary who landed that afternoon and the reception scheduled to take place the next day at the President's Residence.

Victor: "Who is the source of this information?"

Yehuda: "Some Rabbi. My guy in charge of this area says he's known him for years and that he has no doubt that the information he provided is reliable."

Victor: "It's been two hours since you called me. We need to add another hour to the time the source met with your guy."

Yehuda: "I did consider sending a local Jerusalem squad, but this is a Member of Knesset and a prominent figure in the ultra-orthodox community. Too many things can get ugly. I'm also not well versed in this whole Grail thing beyond the coordination center's daily reports which I admit, I only skim through."

Victor: "It's already after midnight. Do you think we can just go and knock on the door?"

Yehuda: "Do you have a better idea? This is your project. I can wait until the morning as far as I'm concerned, but according to the source, there may not be a Grail by morning... if it still exists."

The secret service vehicle stops at a dark spot some fifty yards from the home of the Chairman of the Committee for the Defense Against False Messianism. Yehuda and Victor step out and snoop around. The street is empty and desolate. They walk up and ring the doorbell. A few rings later, the door opens. The Chairman stands in the doorway, surprised.

"Good evening" they both greet him and push their way in. they immediately notice the Grail resting on the table in the middle of the small room. The Chairman watches their eyes. He immediately understands what their visit is about. He charges towards the Grail and throws it into the burning hearth. Victor tries to reach into the fireplace, but the heavy-set rabbi blocks him. Yehuda toils with the rabbi and they both fall to the floor. The rabbi's wife emerges in shock from the bedroom, dressed in her nightgown, and cries "Gevald!!!" pulling on Yehuda's hair as he wrestles with her husband on the floor.

Victor seizes the moment and rushes towards the fireplace. He reaches in with his bare hand and pulls the goblet out of the fire. His palm is burning, and he drops the hot yet intact artifact to the floor. Victor pulls out a police badge.

The Chairman, shouts: "I am a Member of the Knesset. I have immunity...You cannot..."

Victor and Yehuda quickly leave the apartment holding the Grail, wrapped in the tablecloth.

55

At the President's Residence State Hall – the Official Reception for the Holy See's Emissary

Speeches are being made. The President presents the Cardinal with a gift. An elaborate olive wood box. Ilana and Yigal are among the invitees Their eyes are wide open. The President opens the box and shows its contents to the audience – a silver replica of the Seven-Branched Menorah Candelabrum.

The President, says with a smile: "Here, the Seven-Branched Menorah can be received and be brought to Rome without wars or destruction."

The audience laughs. Yehuda and Victor are also standing there. Victor's burned palm is heavily bandaged.

#   #   #

At the end of the ceremony, Ilana approaches Victor.

Ilana: "What happened to your hand, Victor?"

Victor, smiling: " I stuck it where I shouldn't have, yet again. And what brings you here?"

Ilana: "I wanted to see the President give the Pope the Holy Grail."

Victor: "Are you still looking for the Grail? It seems to me that it has already become your Idée fixe. Take a word of advice from an old friend – get over it. Without going into details, I can tell you as a friend... you are wasting your time, and remember you promised to have coffee with me.

56

In the Studio, Ilana and Yigal wait for the Farewell Ceremony for the Cardinal, Broadcast Live from the Airport

Anchorman: The red carpet, the Cardinal, the Prime Minister, all of the dignitaries... the handshakes. The Cardinal is now ascending the stairs of the plane. He waves one hand goodbye. Next to him is the Vatican's ambassador to Israel and the rest of their entourage. Now we see them vanish beyond the door and into the plane.

#   #   #

Yigal releases the air from his lungs: "So, that's it?"

Ilana: "Probably... maybe... but wait..." Ilana jumps to her feet, "I want to show you something."

Ilana plays the tape of the Channel One broadcast from the ceremony that took place at the President's residence.

Ilana: This is when the President presents the gift honoring the Pope's envoy, remember?"

Yigal: "Of course! I was sure that the President was going to pull the Grail out of the box."

Ilana: "Me too, but the ultra-Orthodox would have gone mad if he did that. It would have caused a coalition crisis. Perhaps even the collapse of the entire government. But look here..." Ilana points to a man in a suit standing at the edge of the frame, "...do you know this man?"

Yigal: "Certainly, this is Yosef Dorel, the Executive Director of the President's Residence."

Ilana: "Right, and look what happens now..."

The Executive Director of the President's Residence is caught on camera standing in the corner of the hall, holding a brown briefcase. The camera operator focuses on the President handing the Menorah replica to the Cardinal and their handshake. In the corner of the picture, the Executive Director is seen approaching the Vatican ambassador standing by the wall. They smile at each other like old acquaintances. The Executive Director hands the briefcase to the Ambassador. They shake hands and part ways.

Ilana: "Whoops! There, you see it!!"
Yigal: "He handed him the briefcase."

Ilana, is now playing back the farewell ceremony that was held at the airport a few minutes ago: "And who is holding that briefcase, getting onto the plane?"
Yigal, hesitantly: "The Cardinal?"
Ilana: "Of course."
Yigal: "And are you sure it's the same briefcase?"
Ilana: "I'm a thousand percent sure that there is no coincidence here. But what's in the briefcase?"
Yigal: "What do you think it is???!!!"
Ilana: "Maybe a pair of tickets for the Cardinal and his wife to see Maccabi Tel Aviv vs
Inter Roma in the Euro-cup finals?"

Yigal: "As far as I know, these men are not allowed to marry women."

Ilana, In feigned shock: "Really!? I had no idea."

Yigal: "Okay, so what do we do now?"

Ilana turns off the monitor. She puts on her coat and gets up to go.

Yigal: "Where to?"

Ilana: "All of this has made me thirsty. Superintendent Victor has invited me out for a cup of coffee."

57

Epilogue

Was the Holy Grail in fact flown to the Vatican packed in a brown briefcase? Where is it hidden today? And will it ever be revealed to the public eye?

The diligent investigative reporter Ilana Peres and the senior Police officer Victor Elbar kept their promise to one another and met over a cup of coffee. Though pleasant and relaxed, the conversation offered no help in solving the mystery.

Ilana, eventually, realized that the secret of the Grail is not the main mystery in this strange affair. She tried once again to find Dina the technician from the genetics lab at the Technion, but she had disappeared without a trace.

Ilana thought to herself that if it was indeed the Son of God who drank from the goblet at "the last supper," then it would be a thousand times better for the secret to remain buried forever. Juicy myths are much more powerful and long-lasting than simple dry facts.

#   #   #

So, where and who keeps the data and strange symbols that dotted the sheets of paper coughed out by the genetic laboratory's computer that rose to the sky in smoke and flames?

Perhaps it is buried in the most secret and secured vault in the State of Israel, next to the secret code that would be used to activate the nuclear device (possessed according to foreign sources), and one can not possibly imagine which of these codes in universal, historical terms, has the greater potential for causing damage: the physical-chemical – or the biological-divine.

-The End-

Printed in Great Britain
by Amazon

23216597R00081